Advance Praise

"Patrick Simpson's return to his character Truman Pierce proves that some writers can go back to the well and come up with something completely different. A sharp and satisfying novel that shows growth for both the writer and the character."

— Brandon Barrows, author of *And Of Course, There Was The Girl.*

"Simpson's books inject the rich atmosphere and impassioned, soulful characters of classic noir into a bleak modern world that has become numb to its own corruption"

— Douglas Lumsden, author of *A Troll Walks into a Bar*

"A sleek mystery with vengeance in its blood. Mean, violent, and satisfying."

— Coy Hall, author of *A Seance for Wicked King Death*

"*Reilly* is an action-packed yarn in the pulp tradition. Murder, greed, corruption, and revenge are woven throughout its DNA. In his second outing, janitor-turned-investigator, and a man who can't stop himself from punching up at his own peril, Truman Pierce continues to establish himself as a solid protagonist we want to root for and can't wait to see in action again."

— Whiskey Leavins, author of *Low Angle Shot*

"With echoes of Jim Rockford and Jake Gittes, Truman Pierce winds his way through goons and 9mm's pointed at his head, as he searches for the killers responsible for the death of a good friend. Like his character, Simpson's writing is tough as a gut punch and as clean as a Coltrane solo. One hopes that there are a lot more Pierce stories waiting in the wings."

— Craig Terlson, author of the *Luke Fischer* novels

'Kurt Vonnegut used to warn against disposable background characters. If you get used to characters that don't count, he reasoned, it's easier to separate real life into "important people" who matter and insignificant people who don't. This dichotomy—important human beings versus unimportant human beings—is the most pernicious aspect of today's culture, and a lot of our popular fiction feeds right into it.

Not this novel.

Reilly by Patrick B. Simpson could serve as an antidote to every book that begins with a protagonist who "has it all" until something terrible happens and they have to fight to regain their cushy life, beautiful home, and perfect spouse. The action in Reilly is grounded in a world recognizable to working adults. The characters struggle to make sense of events beyond their control. They try to improve their circumstances. They get caught up in bad situations because they're fallible and desperate.

This is the kind of crime fiction I want more of. An investigator like Truman Pierce whose blue collar experiences feed his insight into human nature. Emotional stakes based on genuine affection between believable characters. And a real sense of what each decision costs. The author's investment in these elements couldn't come at a better time."

— S.P. Miskowski, author of *If You Knew Me*

Reilly

Reilly

A Truman Pierce Novel

Patrick B. Simpson

First Edition

Library of Congress Control Number: 2025948861

Casebound ISBN: 978-1-62720-668-6
Paperback ISBN: 978-1-62720-669-3
Ebook ISBN: 978-1-62720-670-9

Design by Apprentice House Press
Editorial Development by Aminah Murray

Published by Apprentice House Press

Loyola University Maryland
4501 N. Charles Street, Baltimore, MD 21210
410.617.5265
www.ApprenticeHouse.com
info@ApprenticeHouse.com

To my parents,
For letting me soar and not clipping my wings.

1

Bubba Preston was finally handcuffed to the park bench.

David, Goliath, and myself all studied the damages Bubba had done. Fortunately, I only had a cut on my forehead with some blood I was able to wipe away with a tissue I had in my pocket. David rubbed his shoulder like he was putting on ointment, and Goliath had a bump on the side of his head, but that could easily be cured with some beer.

We were in Lansdale Park, witnessing the late evening sun creeping away behind the maple and oak trees. The park was located a few miles from the downtown area, but luckily for us there wasn't anyone out in that part of the park. This area provided the best place for a meetup with Bubba after Goliath pretended to be a senior citizen with information about their 401K.

You wouldn't guess by the six-foot-five-inch Bubba that he was anything but an athlete, but he was scamming people—mostly the elderly—on the internet. He was the type to send you a bullshit notice that either your taxes were overdue or your mortgage payment had lapsed, and then frightening you with eviction and jail time. I would like to think I'd be one of these people he couldn't touch, but my technical skills weren't exactly up to par. He was also not the best with common sense: when we approached him, he started to fight us like we were SWAT.

It had been nine months since the events with Victoria and her merry band of criminals. Seismic shifts in the town were felt when arrests were made and lives were ruined. The police department was the biggest casualty. When the corrupt officers were arrested, it created a staff shortage. You couldn't pay anyone enough to wear the policeman's uniform. They had tried giving bonuses and other perks to get people to apply. I even heard a rumor that the governor was going to force cops from other parts of the state to join the disgraced department.

The guys and myself were hired as consultants to the police department after several months of the station looking like a deserted town. Our job was to go after internet crimes or anything else smaller that didn't involve carrying a gun and busting down a door. It was a job that didn't meet the approval of either Detective Longhorn or Detective Johns, but their higher-ups wanted the community to feel like they were helping fight crime. It didn't take long to understand that me and the guys had become bounty hunters, helping Longhorn, Johns, and the rest of the law-enforcement community catch criminals that had fallen through the cracks.

After David made the phone call regarding Bubba, ten minutes later Longhorn and Johns showed. They were both dressed in their usual cheap suits. Even though Johns was rushing to get there first, Longhorn was ahead of him, looking at me and the others like he was ready to give us detention.

"Jesus, Truman," Longhorn said, quickly moving to Bubba, "I've told you before to stop playing cop; you're on reconnaissance until we show. This isn't going to help you get your private investigator license."

A few months back, I decided it was time to go for my P.I. license. At first, it made me feel like a hypocrite because of my difference of opinion with law enforcement for several years, but things change when someone puts a loaded gun against your head. I might not have had any police experience, but claiming the license by getting recommendations from several law enforcement officers and taking a test that was equivalent to the LSAT was still worthwhile path.

"No," I told Longhorn, unfazed. "This might not help me, but Bubba here did start things first."

Johns, red-faced and breathing hard, spoke as he approached. "Really? Is that also your response to Melvin Anderson?"

"I still say he tripped over the chair," I said.

Longhorn took out a key from his jacket pocket. "Just be more careful. The last thing the department needs is another connection to someone who wants to go outside the law."

"We figured you guys could use the extra help," Goliath said. "You're welcome, by the way."

Goliath had grown some hair on his chest ever since his near-death experience from Victoria's crew. He wasn't hunched over like when I first met him, and he didn't hang his head low when someone talked to him. He didn't give up his wardrobe of heavy-metal band shirts and jeans, but they looked differently with his shoulders back and swagger. Goliath even took time to work out to match his physique with his new confidence.

"We owe you nothing," said Johns.

"Not with the new arrests you've made that wouldn't have been possible without us," said David.

David had been working nonstop helping me pick up a number of these lowlife offenders. He even took time off from school because he thought he could be more active searching criminals than sitting in a classroom. Most of the money he made from each arrest went into upgrading the equipment to help find the perps. I didn't think he could spend more time with his face in front of glowing screens, but then I saw he had a purpose. His enthusiasm about fighting crime was on par with comic book heroes.

"You're still a kid who thinks he is indestructible," said Johns. "Hide behind your computers and gizmos all you want, but you still don't understand how the world works."

Detective Johns was still angry with the world, but he always held back just before he went scorched earth. He rarely spoke on the subject, but you could tell the stained department weighed heavily on his mind. On numerous occasions, he would start to lose his temper, only to start breathing enough to see the red from his face disappear because the sullied reputation of his department meant everyone was now under a microscope.

"And this is how you are treating three people who are helping with your department's reputation?" I replied.

Even with his shoulders back, Johns lowered his face like a disappointed child. I must've used that remark a hundred times, and each time it hit Johns the same way. Johns mumbled under his breath as he handcuffed Bubba and took him away. Bubba tried to get smart with Johns, only for him to squeal when Johns twisted his wrist.

"You should know by now not to poke the rattlesnake," Longhorn said to me as he watched his partner put Bubba in the backseat of their unmarked Dodge Durango.

I said, "Then he shouldn't mess with the mongoose."

He ignored that. "A few names came up in our system. Now, these names are for misdemeanors, so that means you don't have to haul them in for anything. I mean it when I say that if you find any of these wanted people, then contact me or..." He changed his line of thought when he looked towards the Dodge. "Just contact me if you find any of these people."

Longhorn dug through his pockets for a minute before coming

up with a piece of paper that only had six names on it. Longhorn gave me the paper, but Goliath quickly snatched it out of my hand after I held it up to him.

Longhorn said, "Those aren't big time, so I don't expect the three of you to be going on high alert. Just find them and alert the police." He motioned to the car. "And make sure you contact the precinct about payment for—"

"Just did," David interrupted as he held up his phone.

Longhorn shook his head. "Of course. Anyway, all three of you remember what I said. Before I go, do any on you need to be taken to the hospital to get checked out? Those don't look life threatening, but I still needed to ask."

We shook our heads.

"All right. I imagine I'll be hearing from you soon, so don't be stupid and get into more confrontations."

We said nothing as we watched Longhorn stroll down to the unmarked car. He kept his sights straight as Johns wasted no time in airing his grievances to his partner. Having done this routine several times, Longhorn backed the car out of the park without saying a word to Johns. I figured he wouldn't say anything to him until they were on the road.

"David," I said, looking at both of them as we started to clear out, "make sure the department doesn't waste their time trying to wire the money into the bank account. I don't need them to drag their feet like last time."

"Not a problem," he said staring into his phone.

"Do you need a ride?" asked Goliath.

I shook my head. "I want to walk tonight. It'll be good to mentally organize everything we need to do."

The guys said their goodbyes as I watched them jump into David's dark blue Hyundai Elantra. Based on how the car burned rubber getting out of the park, they were eager to start searching the names on the list.

I was happy to have some time to myself. I started to think about what I had to do tomorrow between being a bounty hunter and my obligations as a janitor, and then my mind quickly focused on taking a shower and grabbing a meal. The thought of putting John Coltrane on before passing out sounded appealing, but I was ready to crawl into bed for a much-needed sleep.

It was the start of the longest night of my life.

2

I was around a mile from the park when I regretted not taking the ride with the guys. It was good to manage the tangled thoughts while walking, but it wore out quickly. Luckily, I caught the Number Six bus before it left. It was a forty-minute trip to my neighborhood, letting me off about a half mile away from my basement apartment.

As I walked throughout the neighborhood, I gazed at the "sold" signs in front of several houses. For the past six months, several houses in the neighborhood were being bought up by a real-estate company called Thornton Construction. The houses were similar to the one I stayed in—built in the mid-twentieth century, with land that was easily worth double the cost of the house. I shook my head harder at each "sold" sign I passed. These were homes that people couldn't afford to live in anymore, and Scrooge himself was swooping in and pushing people out.

When I made it to the brick, one-story house where I'd been living for about two years, I saw a faint light coming from the first-floor window. I was surprised to see it because my landlord, Thelma Reilly, was normally in bed by the time the sun ended its work for the day. Instead of going through the walkout basement to my apartment in the back, I went through the front door.

The first floor of the house had exactly what you picture a

ninety-year-old widow would have as furniture and decorations. The chairs and couch had a layer of clear plastic covering them, paintings of dogs and other wildlife hanging on the walls, and other decorative materials either passed down or bought at a yard sale. Even with enough supplies here to make your average Joe laugh, this place felt like home to me.

The light came from the kitchen. I stepped in and found Thelma sitting at the kitchen table. Surprisingly, she was fully awake and cognizant. Her snow-white hair was down, covering part of her face and just touching her shoulders. Thelma wore the same faded light blue nightgown and robe she'd owned since before I was born. She was gazing at a photo album she laid on the table, flipping through slowly as she took in the different pictures. She was so enamored by the photographs that she jumped a little when she heard me walk into the room.

"Oh, Truman," she said startling, "I didn't hear you come in."

"I didn't mean to scare you. I thought you would be in bed by now."

She smiled. "The one time of the year where sleep hasn't taken hold of me early."

I looked down at the photo album. "Reminiscing on old memories?"

"I am," she said, looking down at the album. "Pull up a chair."

I did and noticed on closer examination how well-kept the pictures had been inside the beige, leather-bound album. It looked like each picture was taken yesterday from how clear and undamaged they were. The pictures behind the clear plastic looked as if they hadn't been touched since the day they were put in. Every picture had its own story to tell and Thelma was silently taking in each one.

She turned a page and showed me the wedding photo of her

and her late husband, Henry. Thelma told me she was twenty when she married him. The woman in the photo didn't look anything like the person sitting next to me. The younger Thelma had brown hair, wearing a white wedding dress and a veil to match. Henry was a muscular man of his time, choosing a striped tie to go with his dark suit. Thelma gave a smile I had never seen her give before.

Thelma said, "Henry was nervous the month leading up to the wedding, but that day he was excited. He told me during the ceremony how he wanted to spend the rest of his life with me—and that's what happened. He treated me like no man had ever treated me before. Throughout the years, whatever fights we might've had, I would always see the man in the dark suit matching his eyes on our wedding day."

Thelma had spoken about Henry and her past before, but never at this length. She told me her past the way you would to a biographer or journalist. She picked her words carefully and thought about what she would say next. Thelma smiled as she pointed to another picture from her past that triggered a memory.

She flipped a couple more pages until she stopped abruptly on a photo of her cradling a baby. She appeared to be middle-aged, with a smile as wide as the day she was married.

"Who's the baby?" I asked, craning my head to get a better look at the picture.

Thelma didn't answer right away. Instead, she took her index finger and lightly touched the picture. I knew she'd heard my question, so I didn't repeat myself like so many ignorant young people would do in the moment. I watched as her face went from sad to confused. It was a few moments before she spoke.

"This is my nephew, Edmund," she said, dragging out her words.

"Nephew?" I asked, perplexed. "I didn't know you had a

nephew."

It was no secret that she and Henry never had any children—it just wasn't in the cards. I had asked her when I first started renting the basement apartment if she had any children, but she gave a shake of her head and that was the last time I ever brought up the subject. To see a picture of someone related to Thelma was a surprise.

"Yes," she replied, "Edmund was my sister, Lily's, only child. This picture was taken a week after he was born."

"I've never seen him around here before."

She lightly shook her head. "No, he doesn't come around here anymore. It's been decades since I've seen him. He would be in his forties now."

I went to ask another question, but I bit my tongue when she gave a sigh and turned the page. I just kept watching as she looked at every picture with sorrowful eyes. This seemed more like a time for her than for me, so I started to get up, but halfway across the room she called out my name.

"Truman," she said, closing the album, "I think it's time for me to go to bed." She started to stand, leaving the album on the table.

"What about the album?"

"Oh," she said like she'd just remembered, "I'll put that away in the morning."

I asked her if she needed any help, but she reassured me she had everything under control. I still watched to make sure she got to her room without any problems. When she closed the door to her room, I used the door in the living room to head down into the basement.

In the basement, I took my shirt off and tossed it on one of the kitchen chairs. I grabbed John Coltrane's *Ascension* out of the record collection and put it on the record-player turntable.

Thelma didn't have the best hearing, but I still kept the volume low. My body hit the bed and I was just a few minutes away from sleep. I just wanted to pass out to Coltrane and not worry about tomorrow.

Just as my eyes closed, the rotary phone started ringing. My eyes opened wide like I was hit with an adrenaline shot and made a break for the phone. The last thing I needed was Thelma waking up and asking me what was going on. I took the receiver off the cradle, and then put it to my chest, carefully listening for a moment to see if Thelma had woken up. Satisfied she hadn't, I put the receiver to my ear.

"Yes," I said, "this is Pierce. Who is it?" I couldn't contain the annoyance in my tone.

"Um, yes, Mr. Pierce," said a woman who tried to keep calm, but knew she was frantic. "I apologize for calling you at this late hour, but I had no one else to turn to. My name is Susan Newman and I'm..." She trailed off but only to catch her breath.

"Just take a second to compose yourself and tell me what's going on, Ms. Newman."

I heard her breathe in and out a few times like she was in a meditation class. I knew better than to tell her to rush things and get to the point, but I didn't want to wait the rest of the night for her to arrive at bliss.

"Okay," she said, "I'm ready. Again, I apologize for the late call, Mr. Pierce, but I'm out of options. My sister, Kathleen, has been missing for over a day. I'm worried something has happened to her. Your name has been referenced several times as a person who can track someone successfully."

"Just a day?" I asked. "Doesn't constitute as missing."

"Kathleen and I talk every day and she'd tell me if she was leaving on her own. Something's wrong. It's not like her to go away and not tell me."

"And I'm guessing the police said you have to wait another two days before you can file anything with them?"

"That's correct." She cleared her throat. "I was wondering if you could meet me in front of Kathleen's apartment building tonight?"

"Tonight?" I almost yelled. "Ms. Newman, you must know that searching for someone who has been missing for only a day isn't common. Chances are she's gone out of town for a few days and can't get a hold of you."

"No, I know something is wrong. Please, I have no one else to turn to."

I exhaled. "And what do you want me to do tonight?"

"Help me search her place." I started to speak, but she cut me off. "I have a key to her place. I just want to do a quick run through of her place to get an idea of where she might have gone."

"I wouldn't advise that, Ms. Newman. Going through her place when she isn't there could put us in trouble with the law."

"I have been to her apartment several times. I can prove that by introducing you to the security guard on the first floor. I'll let him know you're my guest and that we're going to my sister's place. We won't be sneaking in nor doing anything illegal."

I went through the different scenarios in my head of what a short notice like this in the middle of the night could mean. Chances are she was telling the truth, but that didn't stop me from being cautious. I was going to tell her, with trepidation, that I would meet her, but she spoke up.

She said, "And I'll double whatever you normally charge for making a call this late."

Again, I didn't just blurt out that I would meet her. I waited a couple of seconds, then told her I would meet her in front of her sister's apartment building in thirty minutes. She gave me the address, and then I hung up.

I grabbed a clean shirt out of my dresser drawer, then proceeded to text David where I was going with a general explanation of the situation, along with Susan Newman's name. He had given me a smartphone, and at first, I couldn't stand the rectangular gizmo, but then got used to it after some time. I figured he would be asleep, but knew he would see the text eventually. I checked around the room once more after grabbing my car keys, and then was out the door.

3

I thought I would pass out the second I got into my Nissan, but when I started the car, I felt a surge of energy run through me. It was the thought of keeping all my senses on full alert for the stranger I was about to meet. My brain went through different scenarios about what might happen and how to escape or neutralize the problem. It was a mental tennis match that kept the hamster in my head running on the wheel.

Since it was the middle of the night, I went on the main roads to get to the apartment complex faster. In the small city, there weren't a lot of people out—just your regular nightshift workers or those giving the nightshift workers a difficult time. I was able to get around without being harassed. The area had a lot of shops and businesses you find in any metropolitan area, but it didn't have all the chaos and energy that came along with it.

Kathleen Newman's ten-story, white brick apartment building was located on the East Side of town. It was a nice area to live in if you were young and still trying to figure out your place in the world. The complex sat next to a small shopping area that included a non-chain grocery store, coffee house, and a couple of restaurants. As I drove up to the complex, I noticed that a few windows still had their lights on at that late hour.

I didn't waste any time as I pulled into the parking lot and took one of the five spaces marked "Guest." My car was pointed away from the building. I looked around the area as I shut the car off. There was no one in sight.

Getting out of the car, I felt a breeze move against my face. The temperature had cooled some, but it didn't make me shiver. The dimly lit streetlights barely touched me and the car, but I wasn't having any trouble seeing the parking lot or surrounding area. Wind blowing was the only noise I heard.

I stood out in the open for a minute, trying to make sense of things. No one was in sight, and I started to thinking someone was putting me on. I went to open the driver's-side door when a woman called out across the parking lot.

"Mr. Pierce!" she yelled multiple times.

A slender blonde moved quickly towards me, like I was already driving out of the parking lot. Her arms were at face level, going back and forth like I didn't already see her. She wore a dark skirt with a blouse and purse to match. When she reached me, she breathed in a few times like she had just done a marathon.

"Sorry," she said, "I thought I saw you on the other side." She extended her hand towards me. "I'm Susan Newman."

I shook it. "Truman Pierce."

"I'm happy you arrived. Listen, we need to get inside as soon—"

I waved a hand between us. "First, I'm going to need you to take a few more breaths and take it down a couple of notches. Getting hysterical isn't going to work for either of us."

Susan did as I said and breathed in and out for a few moments. She even closed her eyes as she inhaled through her nostrils and exhaled through her mouth. It was obvious she had used the technique before. She opened her eyes when she was calm and ready to speak.

"I apologize," she said. "I get like this when I think the worst has happened. I haven't had long to process everything, but I've heard your name several times." She opened her purse. "How much should I pay you?"

I shook my head. "Put that away for now. You don't owe me anything until we know for sure there's a situation to look into."

She kept the purse behind her as we walked into the apartment building. The lobby was smaller than I had pictured it would be as we walked through the glass double doors. The white-tile floor looked to be waxed recently, and more paintings than an art exhibit covered the brown walls. A frumpy security guard who looked to be in his sixties sat on a stool near the elevators. He had his head down, and it was hard to tell with the navy-blue hat he wore if he was asleep, but as we approached, he lifted his head and squinted through a thick pair of black-rimmed glasses.

"Hey, Lou," said Susan. "I'm here to stop by and see Kathleen." She motioned to me. "This is Truman and he's with me."

Lou didn't bother to check the time and just waved us through like it was early afternoon. As we walked towards the elevators, I looked over and saw him lower his head into his previous spot. I just chalked it up to low crime in the area.

The elevator ride up put the spotlight on Susan for me. We didn't say anything to each other, letting me juggle the few things I knew about her. In the lobby, she'd made it sound like I was just a friend of Kathleen. She didn't even bother to ask Lou if he had seen Kathleen, but I assumed that was because he was very forgetful. Still, even with her fidgeting like she did in the parking lot, there was something bugging me about the way she was taking the supposed disappearance of her missing sister. One moment she was frantic, and then the next she played it cool.

We exited on the ninth floor and Susan walked briskly down the hall to door number 907. She didn't bother to knock, but instead she fished through her purse. After a few seconds, she took out a silver key and unlocked the door.

Inside the apartment, the place was cleaner than what I had predicted. A thought crossed my mind that the apartment would be turned inside out. I expected tables and chairs tossed on their sides, papers and other materials scattered throughout the floor, or just some pieces of evidence supporting Kathleen had been in some sort of struggle. What we found was a person who took their time decorating and made sure things were in a specific order.

Susan went left into the kitchen to look at a small stack of mail sitting on top of the counter while I did a panoramic sweep of the apartment. The living room was straight ahead with the vinyl blinds closed. There was a hallway past the kitchen that led off to a number of rooms—all doors were closed. There was a wooden table right before the living room with a daffodil in a crystal vase sitting in the middle. I was looking around, trying to find any clues, when Susan spoke.

"She didn't leave a note or anything," she said, tapping her fingernails on the countertop. "I figured she would. This is another reason why I believe something has happened to her."

I kept looking straight ahead. "Does she have any enemies? An ex-boyfriend that has a grudge against her?"

"No. No one that I know of has anything against her. Her last boyfriend moved across the country last year."

"What does she do for a living? Maybe her absence ties into her job?"

"I can't see why; she's an accountant. She doesn't sell drugs or do anything illegal on the side."

I looked at her. "And you know that for sure?"

"Of course I know that for sure," she confessed like someone had hit her. "She has never gotten into that kind of trouble before.

She's dedicated to her job and doesn't do recreational drugs."

We both looked through the kitchen. I made it a point to lightly go through what I could see and not barge through the drawers and counter space like a madman. Susan, on the other hand, searched through the area with forceful speed. I tried telling Susan to be careful with how she handled Kathleen's possessions, but she acted as if I wasn't in the room. We spent about ten minutes going through the kitchen before I backed away with annoyance.

When my focus turned towards the refrigerator, I took a short time to look over the collage Kathleen had decorated the ice box with. Most were pictures of her and Susan throughout different stages in their lives—from kids to adults in different parts of the country. There was no question they were sisters from their similar physical traits; they both had blonde hair and slender physiques. They only difference I could tell was Kathleen's face looked to be thinner than her sister's. Kathleen also had pictures of exotic places around the world that didn't include her. I assumed these were places she wanted to visit someday.

"Did she have any upcoming trips planned?" I asked as I shifted my sights back to Susan.

Susan abruptly looked at me like I had asked her weight. "No, she didn't have anything planned until later in the year."

Drowsiness started to creep back in, and I felt there weren't any more questions I could ask that could point me in the right direction. Also, there was no evidence to support abduction. I could keep looking through the apartment all night, but my tired state told me I would find nothing of value.

I said, "Get to the police station in the morning if you haven't heard from her."

She took two steps forward with her arms slightly apart. "Wait, you're leaving?"

"There's nothing more I can do tonight, Ms. Newman—"

"Susan."

"Susan. The cops will tell you there isn't anything to do right now without further proof. They can tear this place apart once it becomes an actual case. If she's in danger, then I'll do my best to help."

"Well, let's try her bedroom before you—"

"No. I'm not searching through any more of her apartment before there's concrete proof that a crime has occurred. She could press charges against us for this illegal search, so I'm walking away before anything else happens."

Susan said nothing more. She gave me a nod like she understood, but I felt like she would rather use whatever energy she had left to comb through Kathleen's apartment as opposed to convincing me to stay.

Out in the hallway, there was a moment where I thought Susan was going to run out to tell me she had found a magic clue that would convince me to come back, but nothing of the sort happened. However, I did hear a lot of footsteps and shuffling within the apartment. It reminded me of another sibling obsessively searching for the truth. Vince Hutchins had turned into the violent type, all in the name of finding out what had happened to his murdered sister, Danielle. I was seeing the beginning of that dark path with Susan. She seemed like the type who would do anything for her sister.

At what cost?

4

I thought I was going to pass out in the car as I parked the machine. My legs turned into rubber as I got out of the car and started for the walkout basement in the rear. The temperature had continued to drop since the apartment complex, making me yearn for my bed even more. As I dragged my feet, my tired head lifted and saw a faint light moving inside the house. I lightly cursed under my breath, thinking of all the times I had told Thelma not to wander around the house at night; she wasn't going to know where she was and would accidentally fall over. I shook my head a few times to give my batteries the needed boost to get moving.

I walked onto the front porch, not thinking the door should be locked at this hour until I reached and turned the knob. This realization jolted my senses as I pushed open the door. It was dark as I lightly took a step in.

Quietly, I said, "Thelma, you—"

A fast-moving object hit me in the stomach and my body landed on the floor. I coughed uncontrollably as I held my stomach. I tried to get up, but what felt like the weight of the world pinned me to the ground. I moved my head as much as I could and saw a large man wearing all black and a ski mask holding me down with a baseball bat and his body mass.

"It looks like we have a visitor," he said. His voice sounded like he was fighting asthma.

I lifted my head to find two more men, skinnier but also wearing all-black ski masks and attire, walk from the kitchen. The full moon broke free from the clouds, giving me a better look at the intruders as the light etched through the windows. One of them held a flashlight as the other held a Colt Python .357 Magnum with a six-inch barrel. The light bouncing off the silver made me realize the weapon could cut me in half—even from across the room.

"Where did this one come from?" the gunman asked. The directness in his voice told me he was the trio's leader.

"He just came in through the front door," the big man said.

The one with the flashlight got down on one knee and shone the light directly into my face. I wanted to spit on him, but my mouth was drier than the Sahara. He got so close I could see he had one green eye and one brown eye staring at me. He huffed as he stood back up and looked at the man with the gun.

"No wonder we couldn't find him in the basement," Crazy Eyes said. "I thought he was either hiding or out for the night."

"We know where he is now," said the gunman. He looked at the big man sitting on my back. "He can't move."

None of the voices rang any bells for me or I would've started shouting out names. Each one sounded normal, like something you would hear blended into a packed concert and forget seconds later. Two of them tried to sound tough, but the leader, the one with the gun, had a natural way of speaking. I wouldn't forget his vocal sound moving forward.

The elephant on my back made a grumbling noise as the gunman knelt down in front of me. Even with the limited light from the moon, it was clear I was dealing with someone with an itchy trigger finger. His dark eyes told me he had an agenda that night and no one was going to stop him. He stretched out his arm and calmly put his fingers through my hair like he wanted to make sure I was real. I moved my head, making him grab my hair so I couldn't move. After a moment, he released me and stood up.

"The tenant I kept hearing about," he said.

I coughed. "Just take whatever you came for and get out."

"Oh, I plan to," he said in an almost whisper.

He stepped into the kitchen for a few seconds, and when he returned, he was pulling Thelma forcefully by her arm. Thelma wore the same nightgown and robe I'd seen earlier. She stumbled numerous times, causing the gunman pull her even harder. She was crying, making inaudible noises.

"Get your hands off of her!" I yelled.

He ignored me, pushing her against the wall, next to one of the windows. Her whole body shook, and I was surprised she was able to stand. The gunman kept his hand on her shoulder to keep her standing up straight while the man with the flashlight alternated his gaze between me and his boss.

"Listen," I said, trying to avoid my voice becoming muffled, "she has nothing to do with whatever problems are between me and you. Let her go and take whatever you want."

The gunman laughed like I had said the punch line wrong.

"Truman!" said Thelma, moving her head around like a blind person. "What is happening?"

Before I could answer, Crazy Eyes shone the light on me. When he did, Thelma looked down at me with terrified eyes. I spoke up before she could say anything.

"Thelma, it's going to be all right," I said, trying to push away the fear in my voice. "These men are leaving soon."

She didn't say anything as she placed her hands on her face like she was trying to wake up from the nightmare. Thelma continued to weep, but the gunman shook her like she was a snow globe. The shaking only made her cry harder.

"Do you promise her that?" the gunman asked.

"What?"

"Tell her once more you promise everything is going to be all right."

I took in as much air as I could. I eased my throat before I could speak through the terror in the room. It felt like I was in the Colosseum and the gladiators were circling Thelma and I like hungry crows. I used the darkness to block out the intruders so my focus was directly on Thelma.

I said, "Thelma, we are going to walk out of here. Keep calm and this will be over soon."

The lower half of the leader's mask moved like he was smiling. "You know, I actually believed you."

Thelma whispered louder as the gunman faced her. He stood there for a moment, tilting his head like he was studying her. He lifted the cannon and pointed at Thelma's face. Thelma backed into the wall so much I thought she was going to disappear.

Tears rolled down my face as I pleaded once more. "Please, you don't have to do this. You—"

A bright flash from the gun made me close my eyes. The sound not only rang in my ears but also shook my body.

I told myself to keep my eyes closed because of the bright light, but I knew deep down what would be there once I opened them. I sought to keep my eyes closed forever, not wanting to see the path of destruction lain before me when I opened them. I finally let destiny take hold of me and slowly opened my eyes.

Thelma lay on the ground with half of her head gone. What was left of her face stared right at me. Her right eye was missing, but the left looked directly at me with blood covering it. The remaining mouth had an expression of sadness and confusion. The blood pouring out of her head came at me like a river stream.

I turned into an animal.

I screamed as my body flopped around like a fish out of water. The big man had a difficult time keeping me on the ground as every part of me moved. My bones and muscles turned to steel, giving me the strength to do the one thing I wanted to do to each of the intruders: to kill. My vision had never been so sharp as I looked at each of the three, seeing them clearly and thinking of the different ways I would extinguish their flames.

"Hey!" yelled the big man at me. "Stay still."

I kept showing my rage for a few seconds more until Crazy Eyes came over and helped the big man contain me. Even then, they were still having a difficult time restraining me. It wasn't until the feet of the murderer were a few feet away from me that I showed some signs of calm. All the anger and hate I held inside showed in my eyes as I glared at Thelma's killer. He stood over me like a statue, cocking his head and examining me like he did with Thelma.

He said, "It looks like you didn't keep your promise."

"I'm going to fucking kill you." My contained tone was stronger than any scream.

He lifted the gun and pointed it at my face. Our eyes met and the universe around me ceased to be. If he was going to send my soul into the afterlife, I wanted him to know I wasn't going to show any weakness or fear. I let everything around me go and accepted my fate. I didn't even notice the noise and lights from outside until Crazy Eyes spoke up.

"The cops!" he said as he moved to the window with urgency.

My mind was still on the killer, but I suddenly let my senses rush in. The red and blue lights bounced off Crazy Eyes as he looked outside. The police sirens were getting louder by the second.

The seconds ticked by as me and the killer stared at each other. I wanted to tell him to stop being a coward and pull the trigger already. I could tell from his eyes that this was a born killer, someone who enjoyed watching the spirit fly out of the recently deceased. His finger started to pull the trigger when Crazy Eyes pushed the gun towards the floor.

He said, "Don't shoot. The police cruiser will be here any second. We need to leave now." He looked at the big guy. "Time to go."

The elephant stayed on me, knowing full well the tiger was going to leap at the hyenas the second I was freed. They seemed to be confused about what to do next, and I wasn't going to give them any free advice. Finally, Crazy Eyes grabbed the killer by the arm and pull him towards the back door.

"Come on, Tony," Crazy Eyes said. "We have to go."

The killer, Tony, broke free of him, lifted his black boot, and sent it down on my head. All the lights went out and my senses shutdown.

I'll be seeing you again, Tony, was my finally thought.

5

The first time I met Thelma Reilly was two years earlier as I drifted from town to town, not having the weight of responsibilities drag me down. I had been on the road for over a year at that point, getting as far away as I could from my abusive father. My mother had died when I was a kid, and that sorry excuse of a dad made sure he took out his anger on his only child.

When I had arrived in the small city, I cased it out like any other place I had come across. I had been to rural places and big cities and everywhere in-between, and this place had the mixture of the best qualities from all those places. Crime didn't seem to pop out from every angle, and it was a place you went to when you wanted to lay down roots.

The first thing on my list was to find a place to rent with cash I had saved from several construction jobs I'd worked. Since I didn't own a cellphone, the plan was to go to the library to use one of the computers to search for apartments, but then I came across a flyer in front of a coffee shop. What caught my eye on the xeroxed copy was that someone wrote it in cursive—a practice I thought had died out. The phone number was in big numbers at the bottom of the page.

I went into the coffee shop and laid my dark green duffel bag down beside me as I ordered a muffin and cup of coffee. The barista with magenta hair looked at my stained jeans and ratty T-shirt with disgust. To show I wasn't another street bum looking to steal, I took out a couple of twenties from my pocket. Defeated, she rolled her eyes and asked if I wanted anything else. Putting one of the twenties in the tip jar, I asked if I could use their phone while they put my order together. She gave me an unenthusiastic yes.

I called the number from the xeroxed flyer. The phone rang and rang, and just as I was about to give up, someone answered.

"Um, yes, hello," said a woman who sounded like she was older than electricity.

"Hi, my name is Truman and I'm calling about the room you have for rent."

"Speak up. I can barely hear you."

"My name's Truman and I'm calling about the room."

"I still can't hear you. How about you stop by?"

Without thinking, I told her I would, and then she gave me the address.

When I got to the one-story brick house that afternoon, the woman introduced herself as Thelma Reilly. She wore a sincere smile when she greeted me at the door and didn't remove it the entire time I was there. She wore slacks and a gray sweater that I later learned she'd dug out of her closet and wore for the first time in a few years. She led me into the kitchen where she had chocolate chip cookies and lemonade on the table.

We ended up talking for over an hour. She asked me about my employment status, housing history, and every question a landlord would go over. And I didn't hold back on my answers. I told her I had been moving around for the past year, not staying in one place more than a month. I also told her I had taken a stroll around town when I first got in and wanted to spend some time in the area. I explained I was a good handyman and could help out with maintenance issues around the house. The discussion ended with me getting the basement apartment, with a deal for lower rent in exchange for fixing several housing repairs Thelma had put off.

We sat and ate chocolate chip cookies and drank lemonade for the next half hour like we were grandson and grandmother. She told me about life in the 1950s, reminiscing about her late husband. She laughed and talked like someone who hadn't talked to anyone in a while.

I'll always remember her kind face the first time I met Thelma.

Fast forward to that same face now: half gone and covered in blood.

I sat in the back of an ambulance, holding a bag of ice to the side of my head. I watched from the open doors as the night sky was lit up by bright lights and numerous cops and paramedics who stood in front of them. All the neighbors had come out and tried to get a good look at me through the chaotic crowd. The sounds all around me were giving my headache more of a reason to scream at me.

There were a few cops and paramedics trying to communicate with me at once, but all I could see was their mouths moving. I wasn't deaf; I just didn't have the patience to be answer any questions. I tuned them out because the two detectives I knew were going to show up were the ones I would tell my story to—and only once to the law.

Longhorn and Johns arrived just as my arm was getting tired of holding the ice. They pushed past the cops and paramedics, telling both groups that they wanted to talk to me. You would've thought they were concerned relatives by the way they talked to the uniforms. They stood in front of me, but for a change, neither looked as if they were mad nor trying to teach me a lesson. Even Johns had a face that one might call sorrowful.

"We heard an elderly woman was shot," said Longhorn. He looked around like he was expecting Thelma to appear. "Was it Ms. Reilly?"

I nodded.

"And she's deceased?"

I nodded. All I could do was nod.

Longhorn lowered his head as he turned and went to speak with officers on the porch.

I didn't realize Johns was standing near me until he gave a small cough. He looked at me like I was a child who had witnessed his parents being murdered. His face looked as if Thelma's house had burned to the ground. He mumbled to himself, staring at the house. There was nothing I could say to make the awkward moment turn around, but he opened his mouth and started to speak.

He said, "Thelma was my babysitter growing up."

That unexpected revelation caught my attention. Another kick to the head right then would've been less surprising. I looked at him, ready for anything to make me forget the past hour.

He continued, "My mother knew her from the same church we attended—her and her husband. Whenever my mother had to work late or an emergency popped up, she knew she could trust her six-year-old son with Thelma." He motioned towards Thelma's house. "I was always excited to come here. Thelma always had cookies and a different toy for me to play with every time I showed. She was more like the grandmother I never had. I just...I just don't understand why this happened."

For once, Johns had left me speechless. For a man who acted like he was ready to set the world on fire, he had a side I didn't think was possible. This is what people like Thelma did to people like Johns. The realization was starting to hit Johns much like that boot hitting me in the face. He snapped out of it and stood straight again when he caught me looking at him. He went to say something, but I spoke first.

"When was the last time you saw Thelma?" I asked.

He took a moment before answering, and then said, "A few months ago, at a doctor's office. I was going in for a checkup and she was there. We chatted for a few minutes, and that was it."

I gave a quizzical look. "She was by herself?"

"Yeah. You must've been scrubbing toilets or something that day." He tried to laugh, but ended up clearing his throat like he was trying not to sob.

Longhorn returned a few seconds later. The shock still spread across his face, but he wasn't as jittery. He gave me the cop look that said he meant business, but didn't know how serious I would go answering his line of questions.

"You need to tell me everything that happened, Pierce," Longhorn demanded. "Has anyone spoken to you yet?"

I shook my head. "I think they were waiting for a couple of suits like yourselves to show. They just asked whether I needed medical attention and the possibility of the intruders still being in the area."

"Go through everything you remember."

And I laid out every detail. I told them how there were three intruders. I went into detail about each account of the suspects. First, I gave an illustration of the big man pinning me down and the man with the different-colored pupils. I told them everything about Tony—even his name. I don't know why I told them his name because, before Longhorn and Johns showed, I had promised I would keep that name to myself. But the fact was I didn't have anything more to go on than the name Tony. It even got to the point with my descriptions that Longhorn took out a pad and pen and aggressively took notes.

"Don't do anything rash, Pierce," said Johns.

And then Johns was back to his regular self. He had crossed his arms. I hadn't noticed the stern way he was looking until my eyes found his. Five minutes before that, I had thought he was going to cry, but that was now replaced with resistance. Even Longhorn stopped speed writing and looked at him. Johns didn't wear his normal facial dislike for me; this was what a hard-edged father would give to their teenager.

He continued, "I can see that look on you—the same one as after finding out a loved one died without natural causes. A hound without a leash like yourself is dangerous out there. You'll probably not listen to me, but I still have to give this warning: stay out of the way."

Longhorn jumped into the conversation when the light bulb above his head went off. "Yes, Truman, you shouldn't be involved with the investigation." He flipped through his notepad. "Is there anything else you need to tell us?"

I shook my head. "I told you everything I know. That the person who killed Thelma is Tony, one of the intruders had two different-colored pupils, and the third guy was as big as an elephant."

"You shouldn't say that about someone's size," a voice from behind me said.

I turned and saw a college-aged EMT driver organizing medical equipment. I gave him a look that hit harder than a sledgehammer, and he closed his mouth and didn't add anything more.

I turned to Longhorn and said, "I'm telling you everything that happened." I looked at Johns. "If you think I'm going to quietly sit on the sidelines and pretend the justice system will work itself tirelessly finding the killer and his two stooges, then you clearly don't know me."

"And all I can tell you," Johns said, "is that we can't protect you if you're caught playing vengeful detective. This one requires a badge—not a contract."

I didn't say anything, just took in everything and my surroundings. Johns didn't have me on his list of suspects, but he was still going to keep an eye on me as long as the investigation took. There was nothing Longhorn could add besides the occasional mod.

But there was a lot more to Johns. He threw on the tough cop shield, but once lowered, I believed he was someone who was ready to have a breakdown. He was in his stunned phase, and it was only a matter of time before he started acting like me. He had no problem reminding me that one of us carried the badge, but what was he going to do when he put the badge aside and walked outside the law?

There was commotion with the cops by the yellow-strung tape. I looked over and saw both David and Goliath waving their hands in the air. They were telling the cops they knew me and had to cross the tape to talk to me. An authoritative Longhorn told the cops to let them pass. David had a black backpack slung over his shoulder, while Goliath held a dark brown bag. They looked like their own CSI team.

"We got over here as soon as we heard the address over the police scanner," said Goliath.

Longhorn and Johns said nothing. Johns gave me one more look that said I needed to tread lightly with my next course of action. I could tell he wanted to say something, but knew there wasn't anything more to add besides warnings. Longhorn and Johns both disappeared into the crowd of cops and paramedics, leaving the three of us.

David and Goliath looked around like they were taking in the scene after realizing what had occurred. David was always the first to respond when he noticed one person not present.

He said, "They said something about a shooting. Thelma?"

I nodded.

And like it was on cue, both men went through the bags they brought. Goliath took out his phone and started typing a bunch of things into the gizmo. David went old school like Longhorn and took out a pen and notepad. David seemed to be writing all over the paper with the way his hand was moving fast.

I gave them the same story I had with Longhorn and Johns. Instead of the shocked and low tone I had used with the detectives, I heard myself sound hateful and angry like I did sometimes with my colleagues. As each word of the incident seethed out of me, my body temperature rose. I even found myself repeating the name Tony over and over. When I finally stopped, I gave them a few seconds to catch up before speaking.

"Find out what you can about Tony," I said with resentment.

Goliath shrugged. "It will be difficult with a common name like that."

I said, "This asshole must have a record of some kind. Someone who shoots an elderly woman usually leaves a trail of crumbs."

Goliath went to say something, but ended up closing his mouth and pondered silently instead.

"The physical description of the other two sounds more promising than going off one name," David replied.

"There's no doubt I want the other two, but my search in all of this is to find the triggerman. Just find me Tony—no matter who else you locate."

I stood up, holding my stomach from the pain that wouldn't quit. My head wasn't doing me any justice, but no physical pain was going to keep me there. I looked once more at the house before I turned away from everybody and started to walk. Both guys tried to get me back, but I just kept going.

"Where are you going?" David asked.

I turned to him. "Just find me Tony."

I walked past the cops and paramedics, pushing lightly on the few who didn't see me coming in time. From the corner of my eye, I saw Johns shoot me a questioning look. Him or any of the people in blue would have to tackle and drag me back. I didn't want anyone to keep me around any longer than necessary. I kept my shoulders straight, diverting any attention away from the pain coming from my stomach and head. I didn't know where I was walking towards; I only knew my travel was going to take all night.

I kept walking until the lights faded and night took hold of me.

6

Three days passed and I stood in the local cemetery, watching as they lowered Thelma's coffin into the ground. There was a small crowd gather to watch someone who deserved more from life. The damp ground from the overnight rain made it somewhat difficult for the groundkeepers to lower the coffin. It was midmorning but there was still mist that the sun couldn't touch within the tree line that gave the place a gothic feel.

I wish I could say I made progress finding Tony and snapped his neck, but I spent the majority of those three days at the bottom of a bottle. I turned off the rest of the world and tortured my mind with the realization that I hadn't been able to protect a ninety-year-old woman who had given me a chance when no one else would. My phone would ring with a call or an incoming-text buzz, but I put those problems on pause.

The drinking started the night Thelma was murdered, as I aimlessly walked through town with enough anger to tear down a skyscraper. Wanting to wash down the hate and anger as much as I could, I stepped into a hole-in-the-wall bar on the eastside of town. I wasted no time ordering shot after shot, throwing each back like water and I was in the middle of the desert. People came up to me and I gave them the cold shoulder. After many rounds, I started to fall down and yell how the world was falling apart. When the bouncer wanted to throw me out, I gave him a right hook across the face. The last thing I remember was being thrown out and hitting the sidewalk, making my head and stomach churn worse.

I woke up in the gutter the next morning a few blocks from the bar. I walked home and ended up going through the walkout basement. I made up my mind during my walk of shame that I didn't want to be on the top floor for a while. I hadn't stopped drinking, but I had used whatever sober energy I had to put together the funeral arrangements. I pulled together all the savings I had for the coffin and other services. Thelma didn't have many friends, but I tried calling with the rotary phone as many people as I could remember.

I stood at the foot of Thelma's grave, watching with tunnel vision as the groundkeepers slowly put her into the same hole where we all end up. There were so many things I wanted to say to Thelma, but every time my mouth started to open, I would close it quickly. It wasn't that I had nothing to say, it was that I didn't want to believe my words in the past tense were going to be the last I ever had for her.

Just as Thelma's coffin touched the ground, I looked slightly to the right at Henry Reilly's marker. The married couple was meeting each other after being separate for so long, but not the way anyone had wanted. I even mouthed to Henry my apologies for not protecting his wife like he had while he was alive. Seeing the markers side by side only made the guilt on my shoulders weigh more heavily.

After the service, I drove back to my place—or the horrific crime scene, as everyone was calling it. My hands would start to turn the steering wheel towards the local gin joint, but my mind was strong enough to know there was actual work to be done. I had a lot of missed calls and texts I had to get back to—mostly from

Susan Newman. She had been trying to reach me with more calls and texts than anyone else. I was just going to have to call her and explain that my services were tied up at the moment.

I pulled up to the curb in front of the house, ready to call Susan, when I did a double take and saw the front door slightly ajar. The cops had left yellow "Do Not Enter" tape on the porch, but beyond that I could see the front door was open. I looked around to see if there was anyone else around the house or sidewalk, but no one was in sight. I knew the doors had been locked before I had left for the funeral. Without thinking, I got out of the car.

Please let it be Tony, I thought.

I kept repeating this over and over as my fists balled. There was no rational reason to think Tony would be back, but my hatred for him meant he was the person I wanted to see most on the planet. After last time, I didn't want any surprise from whomever might be on the other side of the door.

When I reached the door, I pushed it with some force and it flew open. I had my guard and senses dialed to eleven as I quickly scanned the area for any surprises. But the only thing I saw was a well-dressed man standing in the middle of the living room, looking around like he was lost. He wore a dark blue, button-down shirt tucked into dark slacks with dark shoes to go with the rest of the outfit. He had his back towards me, but turned when he heard me enter the room. Instead of shock, he gave me a smile like he was expecting me.

"And you must be Truman Pierce," he said as he extended his hand towards me, but I didn't return the favor.

I said, "Even if I wasn't in an angry mood right now, I would still want to know why a total stranger was in my house."

"You have a rented apartment in the basement," he quickly retorted. "This isn't your house."

I moved towards him. "And you're about to be thrown out unless you tell me why you're here."

"My name is Edmund Thornton," he said.

That stopped me. My mind flew to Thelma showing me the baby picture in her album. "Edmund? As in Thelma's nephew?"

He smirked. "Yes, I see Aunt Thelma mentioned me."

"I only heard about you for the first time recently. I guess there was some animosity in the family because she didn't speak of you, but wanted to."

"There was, but I hold no ill-will towards her. That was more to do with my mother and her—the sisters."

"I've never seen you around here before, and I've been living in the basement for a few years now." I gave him a stern look. "Didn't see you at the funeral service either."

He gave me a disappointed look. "To answer both those points: I'm a busy man with a demanding business. It was difficult to spend more time with my construction company as opposed to my ailing Aunt."

"Your construction company?"

He brought back the obnoxious smirk. "Yes, I'm the owner of Thornton Construction."

I sighed. "So, you're the one who keeps buying up all the houses in the area?"

"It's a good time to buy. Real estate is through the roof at the moment."

I went to engage him more about his company when I heard the toilet flush. The bathroom door opened and someone wearing a cowboy costume walked out. The appearance didn't fit him at all. He wore a large brown cowboy hat, but his big head was more distracting. He wore jeans with a black belt and a buckle that had a bull engraved in the silver. It looked like he'd bought it online. But it didn't appear a lot of people argued with him over this, because he towered over me and kept up his appearances at the gym. The cowboy kept the door open, letting the awful smell float throughout the house.

"Mr. Thornton, I told you those enchiladas were—" He stopped when he spotted me.

Edmund smiled and pointed in my direction. "This is Truman Pierce. He was a tenant here."

I didn't like the fact Edmund had put that in the past tense, but I ignored him. Instead, I kept my eyes on the taller man as he walked up to me."

"Hello," he said, extending an unwashed hand, "my name is Tex."

I kept both hands to my side. "That's your real name?"

He lowered his hand. "It's what people call me."

"I'm not calling you Tex. There's nothing about you that says you've ever been to Texas. My guess is you're from the Northeast with that accent you've been trying to conceal. What's your real name?"

Edmund interjected. "Mr. Pierce, I'm guessing you don't know about the upcoming arrangements with the house."

I turned away from the cowboy and gave Edmund a bewildered look. "What arrangements?"

He took in a deep breath. "Well, as you can see, as I am my aunt's only living relative, I stand to inherit this house. Now, I don't plan on keeping this house once I take ownership." He held up his hands. "You will be given ninety days to look for a new residence, but after that time you will be evicted."

I didn't have time to be shocked, so I tried a different approach. "I'll buy the house from you."

He started to laugh but caught himself. "Mr. Pierce, I have

no intention of letting the house stand. I plan on demolishing the building and putting up a new structure. Plus, the land is worth four times more than the house that sits on it."

The few seconds I took trying to think of something to say made the cowboy cross his arms and stand closer to Edmund. He might've been a guy wearing a costume, but he was still tall and looked like someone who wanted to take me in a fight. I could see why Edmund had hired a man like that.

The dead end was approaching and I wasn't wearing a seatbelt. There was no place for me to turn that Edmund and his lackey would agree on. They looked like they were about to leave, so I tried my last shot before they were gone.

I said, "This place meant so much to your aunt. Your uncle built this place himself. There are many memories Thelma had shared with me. I look up and down this street and see all the properties you've bought. You don't need to add this to the foundation of memories you're wiping away. She might've mentioned you in passing, but I could tell she had remorse about not being in your life. Don't let that take away from what this place has meant."

He held up his arms. "I'm sure she was a lovely lady, but I've already started setting in motion a deal to having this place condemned and razed. I hope you do understand: this isn't personal."

"I don't see how I could take it as anything else," I said with hostility.

"Well, I apologize, but I must be leaving; I have a lot of appointments today."

The cowboy created a buffer between me and Edmund as they walked out the door. Edmund kept his focus straight ahead, but the wannabe cowboy gave me a look that begged me to make a move on him or Edmund. When they were outside, Edmund took out his phone and started typing away on the device. No more than a minute went by until a black Ford Explorer pulled up. The cowboy opened the backdoor for Edmund, and then took his place in the passenger seat.

I stood for a few moments in the same spot, sweeping a panoramic view of the house. I wasn't lying about what I told Edmund about the house's history. The only thing I left out was how much the place meant to me. I was trying to keep her spirit alive within the structure, but I also projected my feelings about the place. When I had first arrived, I had pretty much the same opinion of the place that anyone would with a one-story brick house built in the 1960s. But over time it turned into more than I had thought possible. I stood in a place that had turned into a home for me.

I was ready to turn in and pass out on my bed. Adding to the fact that I was going to be homeless soon, my brain couldn't wrap itself around all the painful facts coming at me from different directions. Not even Louis Armstrong or John Coltrane could make me forget the harsh reality.

It was early afternoon when my phone started ringing. Thinking it was Susan, I took the phone out, ready to explain to her why I couldn't help her. I looked at the screen and it was a local number. Normally in this case, I wouldn't hit answer, but my thumb was quicker than my brain. I hit the green button and put the phone to my head. I gave a tired hello into the receiver. A woman with a commanding voice answered.

"Good afternoon. Is this Mr. Truman Pierce?"

I told her it was.

"I'm Sarah calling from the law office of Schutz and Williams. I have Lionel Williams on the line for you."

"What is this about?" I asked.

"It's better if you speak with him directly."

Before I could say anything more, the call was transferred. The line rang for a few seconds before someone picked up.

"Mr. Pierce?" he asked.

"Yes." I kept my voice flat like he was a telemarketer.

"My name is Lionel Williams of Schutz and Williams," he said. His voice sounded like a mixture of wanting to be your friend but also being firm. I wanted to hang up before we had even started the conversation. "I am calling you today because Thelma Reilly left a last will and testament and you name is a part of it. I am letting you know we have scheduled a time for you to come in tomorrow with the others who have been mentioned."

He continued to talk, but my mind was still reeling with the surprise of Thelma writing a will at some point and including me. Why was I a part of this? She'd never mentioned anything to me before and the thought had never crossed my mind. She didn't have much besides the house and everything within the walls. Several questions surged through my head, but I snapped out of it when Williams continued speaking.

"Mr. Pierce?" he asked. "Are you still there?"

"I am."

"Does noon for work for you?"

I thought about how I'd have to leave work early tomorrow, making Henderson even angrier with me, but there was no way I could say no to hearing what would be Thelma's last message for me.

"Noon won't be a problem," I finally said.

Williams gave me the address of the building. I went over the information with him, and then hung up.

I had wanted to spend the rest of the day relaxing and passing out to some smooth jazz, but less than an hour after talking to Williams, I got a call from Susan. When my phone rang, I looked at the number, ready to ignore it for the hundredth time, but I knew I had to speak to her sometime. I hoped she would understand why I couldn't get involved at the moment, but I had to stay firm with my decision. I didn't even get the phone to my ear before she started talking.

"Mr. Pierce, are you there?" she asked, exasperated.

"Yes, Ms. Newman, I'm here. I have—"

"Listen, I've been trying to reach you for some time. It is important that we meet. I have come ac—"

I interjected with my business voice. "Ms. Newman, just wait a second. I have to inform you I can't help you at the time with your sister. There have been personal reasons lately that have come up and I must attend to them. I apologize for not getting back to you sooner."

"But you have to listen to this. Kathleen contacted me yesterday. She was very cryptic with me, telling me not to worry and that she's been moving around lately. She spoke less than a minute before hanging up. I know something is wrong with her."

I took a deep breath. "Then you will have to take this to the authorities, but they will tell you, like I just did, that there doesn't seem to be any danger. She might've been cryptic, but the fact that she contacted you and said don't worry isn't enough for a missing person report and sending out the police force."

"But—"

"Ms. Newman, I'm not going to take on the case. Now, go to the police again and see what they have to say." My voice was stern with shades of annoyance.

There was a moment of silence between us. When she spoke again, it sounded like she was holding back every emotion she felt.

"I see," she said. "Goodbye, Mr. Pierce," and then she hung up.

I dropped the phone on the kitchen table as if it was a pair of keys.

I barely got most of my clothes off before I collapsed onto the bed. I didn't want to think about anything, but consciousness wouldn't give me that break. I started to think of everything from Thelma's death to the house being taken out from under me. The only good thing I could think of was not taking on the Newman case. Adding another boulder onto my shoulders wasn't an option. The more I tried to figure out the other problems, the more my anxiety pressed against my brain, causing a headache that laughed at me. All I could do was let the inner gears start to slowly shut down for the day.

Exhaustion finally won, and I passed out.

7

The next morning, I was back at my janitorial duties at the college, looking at the clock until I could leave. I told Henderson the first moment I saw him that I would have to take a half day. When he started to get pissed with me, I quickly explained it had to do with Thelma, without getting into specifics. It was childish to throw her name out there as a way to get out of work early, but it worked. With an angry face, Henderson told me it would be fine this time, but he was still counting all the days I had missed.

I rushed a day's worth of work that morning. I mopped and scrubbed the bathrooms, emptied out all the trashcans, and even mopped the floors in the science labs. I made small talk with any faculty members that stopped me so they knew I was still employed with the college. If I was going to be at work, then I wanted to make sure that Henderson took notice of all the work I was doing and not get it into his head that I was just doing the bare minimum until I had to leave. I had two strikes against me with the third right around the corner.

During my rounds, I stopped by Danielle Hutchins' old classroom. I was walking by, thinking of Thelma, when I saw that it was now being used as a literature class. I had thought about Danielle now and again, but more so recently after death had knocked on my door once again. It was dispiriting to associate death with

Danielle, but it was the sick way life had burned it into my skull.

As I was getting ready to leave for the law office, David shot me a text saying I needed to get over to his place now. I texted him back what I was about to do, but he kept insisting. I finally told him I would be over there the moment I left the law office.

I changed and was starting to head out. Henderson sat behind his metal desk, going through work orders that seemed to be stacking higher than he could finish processing them. I stood next to his desk so he could see me leave and not forget later.

"I'm leaving now," I told him, "but I'll take most of those orders from you when I get back."

He gave a huff, and then said, "Don't let Thelma's death become an obsession." His voice was soft, but seemed to echo throughout the room.

I looked down at him. "What do you mean?"

"Your determination, Truman. I saw you do the same after Ms. Hutchins was murdered. Terrible things happen every day, but that doesn't mean it can tear apart what we stand for. You're too young and smart for that path, even though you're completely hardheaded."

I faked a smile. "I know I haven't been around to work much lately, but when the dust settles, I'll make sure to pick up the slack."

He shook his head, focusing forward. "That's not what pisses me off. You're a good worker, but you put too much onto yourself." He gave himself a moment before speaking again. "This isn't the first time I saw the same devotion break someone down."

I stood there for a few seconds, waiting for him to say more, but it didn't happen. He didn't seem to be waiting for me to reply, and I had to get to the will reading, so I told him goodbye and that I would be back soon. I heard his sigh as I walked out.

The law office was on the other side of town in the business district. I don't normally drive across town during lunch hours, and this was evident as I got stuck in some traffic. I was going to run a little late, but I didn't think the whole world would crash if I was casually tardy. I watched as the suits and skirts rushed out of their high-valued places of work to try and get food or whatever errands they had to do in their sixty-minute break.

When I pulled up to the seven-story building of Schutz and Williams, I saw two valets out front next to the basement garage. One of the valets got into a gray Mercedes and drove it into the garage. I pulled up to the second valet, and I knew by the way he looked at my car that an excuse was coming my way. He walked over to the driver's side with a judgmental face as I brought the window down.

"Hello, sir," he said as he changed his expression to professionalism. "I'm sorry, but I'm about to go on my break." He motioned towards the garage entrance. "You can park your car in there. Sorry for the inconvenience."

Saying nothing, I pulled away quickly, making him jump back a few feet.

Once I parked the car, I used the elevator in the basement to go to the top floor. The hallway had oak walls and green-carpeted flooring that took me all the way down the hall to the double-glassed doors with "Schutz and Williams" in big, black letters. I opened the door and took notice of the wide variety of flowers throughout the waiting area. There was a coffee table in front of four dark-wood chairs with three vases of white roses, lilies, and carnations. The reception desk had four vases filled with flowers in a row. I pushed one to the side and found a brunette receptionist. She jumped a little when she saw me.

"Hello," she said, composing herself. "Welcome to Schutz and Williams. How may I help you?"

I told her my name.

"Yes, Mr. Pierce. They just started." She pointed to a door marked Lionel Williams, Esq. "You can go in."

I didn't knock as I entered and almost hit someone in the process. The room was bigger than I had anticipated, but filled with people. All eyes were on me as I was the last to arrive. The entire room was made up of suits and skirts. Wearing jeans and a T-shirt, it hadn't occurred to me before now to dress up for the occasion. I could feel all their eyes on me as they each judged me for my appearance and tardiness. At the front, sitting down in black leather chairs, were Edmund and the cowboy. Both smirked at me like two bullies in the high-school cafeteria. Through the sea of people, I saw a man with salt and pepper hair and a dark mustache behind an oak table. He squinted at me, and then spoke up with recognition.

"Are you Mr. Pierce?" he asked.

I told him I was.

"Okay, good. I'm Lionel Williams. Make yourself comfortable and we can begin with the reading."

As he started to read the will, I looked around the room, amazed at how there were more people listening to the will reading than at the cemetery for Thelma's funeral. They stood around like it was a church service, listening to the gospel of possessions, hoping to collect whatever items she'd left behind. I had never met most of the people in the room, and they surely had never stopped by for a chat with Thelma during the last two years she was around.

"And to Truman," said Williams.

I snapped at attention and focused.

He continued, "Truman, you were always someone I could rely on and I was proud to call my friend. You were there for me and didn't judge me whenever most people did. In the time I got to know you that was more than I could say about any of my family and so-called friends."

I gazed around the room and caught most of the crowd forcing themselves to hide their embarrassment and continue to smile.

Williams went on. "That is why I am giving you the house and all of my savings—valued at close to a half-million dollars. You can use that to build the life you want for yourself. You always had the potential to do something. Now you can."

Williams kept talking, but I couldn't get away from all the eyes in the room burning into me. The way everyone mentally judged me when I walked in turned into a room of people who now saw me as the enemy. People with deep pockets whose entire lives revolved around making money and stabbing people in the back were not the ones you wanted to make enemies with. Most of them hadn't known me before today, but they were going to walk out with my name branded into their brains. I was afraid I would have to outrun the rich mob.

"And to my nephew, Edmund," Williams declared.

All heads turned back to the lawyer, trying to find any hope.

"Edmund, I never got to know you like I wanted. Maybe I should've made more of an effort to get to know you, but it didn't seem like you were interested."

I looked over at Edmund. He shrugged and smiled like it was a punch line.

"But I still wish you well. That is why I am giving you a picture that has meant so much to me. Take this with you and cherish it the way I did."

Edmund groaned as the lawyer pushed a few papers out of the way to retrieve a four-by-six picture. I could only see the backside of the photo as Williams reached across the desk and handed it to Edmund. Without looking at the picture, Edmund stood up and reluctantly took it with him. Edmund signaled to the cowboy that he wanted to leave. The duo pushed people out of the way as they tried to make a getaway. Edmund couldn't resist as he stopped a few feet from me and gave me a crooked smile.

"Well, Mr. Pierce," he said, "you got what you wanted." He lifted his hand when I tried to speak. "What other services were you providing to my aunt?"

I kept my cool. "I didn't know Thelma had any will, especially one with my name on it. If you want to discuss this some—"

"I knew you were fixing up the house, but I didn't realize you were also providing additional services that made her fork over everything she owned." He said the last part with a smirk.

I took a step towards him, but the cowboy put his arm out between Edmund and I. The cowboy gave me a look that told me to try it, and I returned the same back at him.

They knew this was going to lead nowhere good, so they kept walking. I watched as they marched like pissed off teenagers into the reception area. At the reception desk, Edmund looked at the photo he was given for a few seconds before dropping it. The photo hit the rim of the trashcan and fell to the floor. Edmund and his guard said nothing as they walked out the double-glassed doors.

After the reading, Williams asked me to stay as everyone filed out of the room one-by-one. I knew I wouldn't be playing poker with them anytime soon by the hate in their eyes and their facial expressions. When everyone was gone, Williams asked me to shut the door. I obliged. I stood in front of his desk, not wanting to sit in the chair Edmund or the cowboy had just occupied.

"That went as well as expected," Williams said with a nervous smile. He dug through some papers before pulling out a few and laid them before me. "Here is the deed to the house. You are going to have to sign it and these papers for a money transfer. The half-million is not tax-deductible. Normally, once we have your banking information, it will take around thirty days before you see the money in your account."

He handed over the papers I needed to sign. I looked them over, pretending I understood what the legal language meant as my eyes glossed over each word. I signed in the areas that needed the black ink. I didn't have much to begin with, so I didn't see any reason why the lawyer in the two-thousand-dollar suit would take away my janitor's pay. After signing the papers, we shook hands and I started for the door.

As I walked out of Williams' office, I looked at the picture Edmund had dropped onto the ground. I picked it up and observed it. It was a copy of the picture of Thelma and baby Edmund. I looked at the picture of her holding Edmund in a new light. Before, it was of a young woman holding what would become, the only relative she had left on the planet. Now, I saw it as a getaway to a past Thelma had wanted to experience once more. I understood looking at the picture why that hadn't happened to her again. I put the picture in my pocket and left the building.

Outside, my phone started buzzing. I took it out and saw David's number flashing in big letters. I hit the green button and put it to my ear.

"Truman," he said without letting me getting a word in, "you're going to need to get over here."

I sighed. "If this is—"

"I have information on Tony."

Me and rest of the world around me stopped.

"Well, sort of," he said.

"What does that mean?"

"It's a lot to explain, but I'm at the apartment with Goliath."

I hung up. I rushed out of there so fast in my car that I didn't even bother to give the valet a sarcastic response.

8

David and Goliath's apartment was above a Chinese restaurant on the West Side of town. The structure had been there for a few decades. The neighborhood was on the line between good and bad neighborhoods, but that didn't stop them from each getting out of their parents' houses and jumping into the real world. It was an area I could live in, but didn't exactly walk around in freely at night. After taking down Victoria's crew and picking up contracts with the local department, the guys thought it was time to move on. They couldn't afford much, but that didn't stop their determination to be independent.

When I parked my car in the free-parking garage across the street, I walked into the restaurant, made a right at the door and walked up the stairs. The smell of General Tso's chicken and spring rolls stayed with me all the way to the second floor. There were two apartments on the right side and I knocked on the second door gently.

Goliath answered after shuffling his feet towards the door. He ushered me though the kitchen and into the semi-large living room. The room was covered with enough electronics and machines to make the CIA blush. Granted, a lot of the equipment was used, but they took care of them like they were their babies. Each guy had their own computer station with multiple screens, self-made desktops, ergonomic keyboards, and each with their own leather chair you could sleep in. David hunched to the right as he stared into one of the many screens glowing in his face.

"Would you like a drink?" asked Goliath.

I shook my head.

David turned to me, blinking to adjust his eyes after the bright screen. "Hey, I didn't hear you come in. Did you want a drink?"

"Goliath already offered." I pointed towards his computer screen. "What did you find?"

David motioned me over to his desk. There was a brown-cushioned chair a few feet away that I pulled next to David and sat down. He shuffled through a number of papers, quietly cursing. I glanced at the computer screens. I recognized a few locations, but others I couldn't make out off the top of my head.

He said, "So, I didn't find anything on this Tony yet, but—"

I stood up and started to walk towards the exit.

"Where are you going?" David asked.

I turned to him. "I made it clear I'm looking for the gunman. It appears you have a number of locations on the screen turning into a maze. I want the exact location of that murderer."

"You're right. I know you want to find Tony, but I have the next best thing: one of the intruders."

He gave me a smirk because he knew I wasn't satisfied yet. Sighing, I made my way back to the chair, half facing him and the computers. I leaned back, watching as he continued to shuffle his papers.

"So," he said, "we went back and searched the criminal database for names and aliases with the name Tony. As you can imagine, the system spit out more than anticipated." He motioned towards the screens. "We then tried to limit it to the surrounding area, using Tony as a nickname. We even reduced it to armed robberies and homicide, but still nothing came up."

I was growing impatient again. "And how does this find one of his accomplices?"

Goliath walked over and handed me a manila folder. I opened it and the big man who had sat on me during the break-in looked at me from his mug shot. He had thinning hair, pale skin and it looked like he was breathing heavy during his mug shot. His light blue eyes stared at me the same way they had the night Thelma had died. Put a mask over the pudgy face and I knew it was the same person.

"His name is Stephen Williams," said Goliath.

David said, "It was blind luck that we found him. We were so busy looking for this Tony that we haven't really had time to delve into the other two. We came across Stephen when we were looking at crimes like larceny and theft in the area. Goliath found him from the recent petty-larceny charge he had on file. He's served some time, but nothing major."

David kept talking as I studied the picture. I knew this low-life was the key to finding Tony. The anger I had that night kept escalating within me. I didn't realize how long I had been studying the picture until I felt a hand on my shoulder. I looked and saw Goliath peering at me.

"Lost you there for a moment," he said.

"I didn't expect to find out anything about the intruders this soon," I quickly replied.

Goliath's concerned face didn't change. "Is that it? It looked like you were mentally going to a place one goes to for revenge. I thought your eyes were going to turn red."

"It's hard not to after what happened."

Goliath nodded. "Understood, but letting your emotions dictate your next move can bring you down."

I smirked. "Since when did you become an expert on revenge and mental stability?"

"I've had my fair run-ins with the bad side."

I could've gone with another sarcastic remark, but the man was right. The soft look in his eyes gave me some comfort. I should've known better than to keep the emotions at bay instead of thinking of new ways to hurt each of the intruders. Mistakes were already being made, but there was still time before I tripped into my own grave. I took in a couple of breaths before continuing.

"What's the address on this guy?" I asked.

David hesitated. "Maybe we should call Detective Longhorn."

"Just so this Stephen can deny everything and walk away without breaking a sweat." I shook my head. "No, I changed my mind. I need to see this bastard's face. He'll talk when it's just me and him."

"How about we come with you?" asked Goliath.

I looked at him, unblinking. "I promise you I'm not going to kill him. Yes, I have anger in me, but that doesn't mean I'm going to be thrown in prison for the rest of my life because I can't control myself. I will rough him up if he tries a fast one or looks at me wrong. I'm not going to throw it all away on the first perp I find."

"And how does this all end?" asked David.

I wanted to tell them it would end when all three were in jail, but my mind had a split-second vision of each intruder in their graves. I didn't mean for that thought to creep into my head, but my subconscious wouldn't give up. It was something that I couldn't deny enjoying, but I also couldn't let the thought camp out in my mind for long. Ultimately, I changed the subject.

"I need you to look up a couple more people," I said.

Both looked at me like I was going to run naked into a bank with only a water pistol and rob it.

"I need information on Edmund Thornton. He's the owner

of Thornton Construction, and happens to be Thelma's nephew. Also, he has a bodyguard who goes by Tex." I said the name with reluctance. "Find out what he does for Edmund and his real name—*especially* his real name."

"Why do you need information on them?" David asked.

I went through all the details with them—starting with my first encounter. Both David and Goliath made questionable faces like someone would do when they heard about a rich, pompous nephew and someone dressed as a cowboy. The guys could tell I was dealing with people that were more than sketchy.

My story then took a right turn into the law office and the will reading. Both of their expressions showed shock. Goliath had to take a seat. It still didn't register what Thelma had left for me as I described the occurrence like it was a dream I'd had the previous night.

Goliath whistled slowly. "I can see why you want information on them. You have a bullseye on your back for the wrong people."

"And they'll drag it out for years, if they have to." I looked at David. "Find what you can about that construction company. They are buying up neighborhoods like candy and don't seem to be slowing down."

David put his face back into the computer screens like he hadn't moved, and Goliath got up and paced around the room. Each had their own way of processing a hard drive full of information.

I got up from my seat. "Text me Stephen's address, David."

"You're going over there now?" he asked.

"I'm not going to wait until Christmas for my gift."

He lightly nodded. "Okay, will do."

Just as I got to the door, out of instinct, I turned. Goliath stood a few feet away. His mouth was closed but the rest of his face spoke volumes. I forced myself to give him a small smile like I'd heard a bad joke, but his face didn't change. Instead, he walked up to me as my hand touched the doorknob.

"Are you sure I can't go with you?" he asked.

"No. I meant what I said about this consuming me. I'll be in contact later once I get some information."

He nodded, but it wouldn't fool a blind man. Goliath still had questions and concerns with me, but I didn't want to stay another hour for any unwanted therapy sessions. I walked out the door before any more awkwardness could ensue.

I spent over thirty minutes driving to the trailer park that David had texted me. The place was outside of town, but it still didn't need to take so long to get there. I told myself I was using the time to wait for the sun to set, but the real reason was I needed to get my thoughts straight and prepare for anything. My mind calculated if he was by himself, how many people would possibly show, what type of danger I would be in, and so on. But the big question I kept asking myself was about the chances that I'd find Tony there with Stephen. The odds were slim, but there was still the chance of laying down a full house.

Across the street from the trailer-park entrance, I parked my car into the parking lot of a small shopping center. I made sure to park at the far end that was empty. The thought of just driving on the bumpy dirt ground through the trailer park wasn't the best course of action. I wasn't sure where Stephen's trailer was located, and I didn't need him spotting me from a distance. I sat in the car for about fifteen minutes, staring at the entrance to the trailer park as the sun started to say its goodbyes for the day.

After taking a deep breath, I got out and walked towards the entrance.

9

The layout of the trailer park had no rhyme or reason to it. The trailers were scattered throughout the area like they had been dropped from the sky. The light from the sun was weak, but it moved through the trees, giving off just enough light within the area. The ground was partially muddy, even though it hadn't rained that day. I made sure to be careful where I stepped.

Some of the occupants gave me dirty looks as I walked the uneven grounds, but most didn't notice me or didn't care; they probably thought I was a resident in their community. I kept my head slightly down, but noticed that, even on a relatively cool evening, most people were outside of their trailers. One man sat on a plastic lawn chair in front of a gray trailer with a woman screaming at him from the trailer window to come inside. Near another trailer, I witnessed a woman throwing out a number of clothes and other items in a rage, telling her partner that he should've thought twice before sleeping with her sister.

I must've walked around for about twenty minutes, thinking David had been mistaken on the whole ordeal, when I spotted Stephen. He stood out front of a rustic trailer in a tank top and jeans, smoking the remains of a cigarette. The light from his trailer cast a spotlight on him, giving me a clear picture of the person I was looking for.

I moved behind one of his neighbors' trailers, making sure he didn't see me. When I looked around the corner, he kept his focus forward. He looked to be completely oblivious of anything. As he blew a cloud of smoke into the air, he would follow the white smoke until it dissipated into the night sky. His face wore a disgruntled look as he flicked his cigarette to the wind, turned like someone was yelling his name, and waddled back into his trailer.

I came out from the shadows, walking carefully on the soft ground. There was no reason to think he could hear my feet on the grass, but I wasn't going to take that chance. I occasionally looked around like somebody was going to jump me. When I made it to Stephen's trailer, my fist gave three soft knocks against the door.

"Is that you, Becky?" he said. Feet shuffled alongside a number of items hitting the floor. "I didn't think you would show. I've got the handcuffs rea—"

When he opened the door, it didn't take longer than two seconds for his face to register shock. I kept my neutral face but clenched my fist.

"You!" he squealed. It wasn't a question but recognition.

I punched him right above his nose, sending him back a few feet into the trailer. Quickly, I stepped inside the trailer and closed the door. He flopped on the floor, trying to get up. I kicked him in the stomach, then placed my foot on his chest to keep him in place.

"How did you find me?" he asked, covering his face.

I ignored him and looked around the room. The place could've had a dozen maids and it still would've taken a year to clean. The kitchenette had utensils and paper plates scattered on top of the counters, different stains covering the stove and sink, and more trash on the floor than actual flooring underneath. What little furniture he had was covered in stains and cuts. Under a fast-food wrapper on a brown coffee table was a pair of fuzzy, purple handcuffs. I grabbed the handcuffs and put them in my pocket.

Holding onto Stephen's arm with both hands, I pulled him with every muscle and bone my body could afford. Stephen cursed, saying how he was going to kill me. Several times he turned into a statue as I kicked him, and he went limp. My body felt like it aged twenty years pulling the blob a few feet to the stove. When I did, I took the handcuffs from my pocket, put one around his wrist and the other to the oven handle. I wiped my forehead with my arm, feeling like I had done a triathlon.

I said, "I don't want you to surprise me again and sit on my back like a coward."

He spat at my feet. "Tony should've shot you."

I smirked. "Speak of the devil. I want you to tell me everything you know about Tony."

Instead of giving me the facts, he started to laugh like I had told the funniest joke. He gazed at the fuzzy handcuffs, keeping his mouth open. He coughed a few times as he looked back at me. I kept my look stern the entire time.

"I'm not telling you shit," he said.

Without wasting time, I walked over to his hand in the handcuffs, took his pinkie finger, and snapped it. He started to wail, wiping away his grin. Terror replaced it. He pulled on the handcuffs, acting as if they were made of plastic, but then reality hit when the cuffs tightened around his wrist.

I wasn't sure how far his screaming would travel before curious neighbors came knocking or called the cops. While Stephen kept flailing, I looked through the cracks in the window shade to see if there were any movements. After around ten seconds of no one rushing up to the trailer or screaming anything at us, I felt a little at ease. I hoped stuff like that was commonplace around the trailer park and people knew it came with the territory. I looked away from the window and down at Stephen when he ran out of breath to scream.

"Look," I said," if you think I'm going to be hanging out here all night, waiting for you to give me small bits, you're mistaken. There are plenty of bones to break and I'm only getting started."

Sweat dripped down Stephen's head, but he said nothing.

"Good, I was hoping you would make this more fun for me." I started towards him.

He lifted his arm in a stop motion. "Wait! Don't hurt me anymore. I'll talk."

"Tell me everything about Tony."

He huffed. "I don't know anything about him except his name."

"Wrong answer." I took a step towards him.

Stephen moved his entire body this time in self-defense. "No, really, I don't know anything about Tony expect for his name. The other guy with us that night knows Tony. I was brought in at the last minute. I didn't even meet Tony until that day, and I haven't seen him since."

I took a few steps back, lifting my head to the ceiling. Not the answer I was looking for, but it gave me something I didn't know before. Stephen had a look on his face that said he would've given me the combination to his safe if I'd asked for it. I had no reason to think he was lying, but I was hoping for more. I would get as many details as I could before I left.

"What does Tony look like?" I asked.

He shrugged. "Just like some regular guy. He's got brown hair and brown eyes."

"Any distinct features?"

Stephen gave me a puzzled look.

I rolled my eyes. "Anything like scars or tattoos that would stand out?"

"I didn't study the guy's appearance before we did the job. He had a trimmed beard. Just a regular Joe you would see on the street."

"Tell me about Crazy Eyes," I commanded.

"Who?" he asked. His face made the baffled look again.

"The person who got you involved in all of this—the third person that night."

"Oh yeah, I forget about his eyes sometimes." He took in a breath. "His name is Darren."

"I'm not interested in just first names. What's his whole name?"

He sighed. "Darren Carver. I've known him for a few years. We've done a couple of jobs together."

I nodded. "And where can I find this Darren Carver?"

He shook his head. "If I tell you, then I have a lot worse coming my way; they'll do more than just kill me."

I knelt down, reaching over to his hand in the 'cuffs. He squirmed, telling me to stop and not do any more harm. I paused within an inch of his hand. I peered down at him, not speaking until his eyes met mine.

"Not as much damage as I can do to you," I said. "You'll only wish you were dead after I break some more bones." I grabbed his wrist with one hand and all his fingers with my other and started to twist.

"All right, stop!" he screamed. "Darren lives in an apartment building on Cypress Street in the downtown side—forty-four-twenty-two. Normally I meet up with him there or here."

I let go of his fingers and wrist, moving back slowly until he saw my face.

"So, what now?" he asked. "Are you going to do more damage?"

I squatted low enough so that he knew we were on the same level. "I'm going to uncuff you, and then you are going to turn yourself into the police while I have a chat with your pal, Darren."

He scoffed. "Turning myself in? And why would I do that?"

"Because I'm going to do more than just break you physically. I'll make sure the entire world knows your face better than Osama bin Laden and Lee Harvey Oswald. I'll have your image and your crimes all over every website and social-media outlet there is. Wherever you go people will spit on you and call you a murderer. Setting up an igloo in the North Pole won't do you any good. If I can't get to you, then I'll pay people to beat the shit out of you so bad you'll never leave the hospital. But you'll always be alive with just enough cognitive dissonance to know why your path led you to that point. Prison? I'll make sure there are enough gang members and rapists meeting you in the showers every day. I'll call in every favor anyone has ever owed me." I took in a breath. "Now, tell me what you're going to do when I leave."

Stephen had not made a sound the entire time. He glided his eyes around like he wanted to wake up. He wiped the glistening sweat on his forehead before he opened his mouth.

"I'm going to turn myself into the police." He had to take in several deep breaths like he had been at the gym all afternoon.

I nodded. "Where are the keys to the handcuffs?"

He motioned towards the top of the refrigerator.

I stood up and reached on top of the fridge. I felt around for a few seconds, disgusted by the trash and dirt my fingers were touching. When I landed on the metal key, I pulled it off the top, but in the process pushed a number of objects off.

I started to wipe my hand on my jeans when I looked over and saw a picture that fell onto the counter. I picked it up to get a better view of the colored photo. My eyes squinted until the lone person in the photo was clear to me—Kathleen Newman. It wasn't the same picture Susan had shared me with me, but I still knew it was her sister. In this photo, Kathleen stood in front of a white wall with her head slightly turned.

"What are you doing with this picture?" I said to Stephen as I smacked him across his face.

He rubbed his face as he studied the photo. "Just some dumb bitch I was paid to find."

"Was it Darren who gave you this?"

He said nothing.

I took his ear and started to pull. I was filled with enough energy that I actually thought I could rip the cartilage off his face. He screamed, begging me to stop. I only eased off a little.

"Okay, all right," he said. "Yeah, I got it from Darren."

There was no point in asking him anything more since he was only the dunce who tagged along on jobs. Not only was Darren on my radar, but my search for Kathleen was put back on. I tossed Stephen the key as I started for the exit.

I said, "I better hear you're at the police station within the hour. If not, I'll have you broken before dawn."

He sat like a decomposing pile of lard, shaking his head that he understood me.

I pocketed the picture and slammed the door behind me.

10

Still in the trailer park, I got my phone out and frantically called Susan Newman. My head and body shook in unison as I kept getting Susan's voicemail. I cursed every time Susan's voice told me to leave a message. It got to the point where people were looking out their windows and giving me nasty stares as I sprinted between trailers and out of the park.

I gave up on Susan and called David. The phone kept ringing and ringing, but I wasn't going to let up. I had gotten to my car when he picked up.

"Hey, how did it go?" he asked.

I ignored his question. "I need you to track down an address for me."

"How urgent?"

"A week ago," I replied.

Shuffling and muffling on the other line proceeded for the next minute. David clicked on a keyboard, mumbling that the damn machine wasn't fast enough. There was a quiet pause before he continued.

"Okay, what's the name?" he asked.

"Susan Newman. The sister of the missing woman I was looking into a short time back."

David started to say speak, but stopped and went about typing away on the keyboard. He switched over to speaker as he continued to type away. As I heard David trying to find information, Goliath's voice beamed from the background.

"Is that Truman?" he asked David.

Before David could answer, I spoke up. "Yeah, it's me."

Goliath's voice moved closer to the phone. "What happened? What's going on?"

"Stephen will shit his pants before he commits another crime again, but right now I need to find the address on Susan Newman." Goliath started to speak, but I cut him off. "I'll explain later. I need the address first."

Only the sounds of car engines nearby distracted the three of us. After a few seconds squirming in my seat, I told David to text me the address, and then hung up. I put the car in drive and stomped on the gas pedal.

I kept my hands gripped around the steering wheel, waiting for my phone to ding with Susan's address. I started to think the asphalt would turn into a yellow brick road and I would be transported to Susan's place. My reasoning was that I wanted to point the car in the right direction when I got the text, but in reality, I couldn't get the worst possibilities out of my head. I wanted to tell Susan that there was more to the story and I was going to find out what was happening.

The phone buzzed in the passenger seat when I was at an intersection. I looked at the address David had texted. It hit me when the address I was staring at was only a mile away from Kathleen Newman's apartment complex. I made an illegal U-turn, pissing off drivers as they honked at me. I kept going as I made a quick shot across town.

The address David sent was also an apartment building like Kathleen's, but the four-story concrete structure was nothing like her sister's. The place looked older and more rundown. The faded exterior walls looked as if they were constructed in the seventies. There was more graffiti on the sides, but the owners of the apartments looked like they tried to keep up with appearances as much as possible. I parked in front of the building, next to a fifteen-minute parking sign.

When I entered the building, I started to check the first floor for a super or someone who could guide me into Susan's apartment. There were stairs and an elevator to the left and a hallway with dark brown walls and linoleum floors to the right. Luckily for me there weren't many doors to choose from and one door that wasn't labeled. I knocked on the door multiple times, making sure I didn't bang too hard in my excitement. Without missing a beat, a voice told me to wait a moment. The door opened and a lanky man with thick glasses peered at me with giant brown eyes. His green T-shirt was on backwards and his jeans were too tight.

"Yes, can I help you?" he asked with hesitation.

"Are the supervisor of the building?"

He nodded.

"My friend, Susan Newman, has been very depressed lately about her sister Kathleen, and now she isn't answering any of my calls or texts. I need to do a wellness check on her."

I didn't have time to tell him the truth, nor did I think he would believe anything I would say. I was looking at someone in their thirties, giving me a quizzical look as he pondered what I'd said. I was surprised he didn't follow my quick request with a line of questions. Instead, he gave me an unamused nod.

He said, "Give me a minute to grab the key."

We rode up in the elevator to the third floor without saying a word to each other. He kept looking over at me, giving me a stare like he was questioning the situation. When we exited on the third floor, he led the way down a hall identical to the first. We got about two-thirds of the way when he turned to a door marked 306. He knocked twice.

"Susan, it's Larry," he said. "Got your friend out here who wanted to check in." He waited a few seconds before knocking again.

I grew impatient, but I kept my body language neutral. I was ready to kick the door in when Larry started to reach for the doorknob.

"Susan, we're coming in," he said.

Larry's face looked worried when he turned the doorknob without unlocking it. He slowly pushed the door open, calling Susan's name out in a low voice. He hadn't pushed the door all the way when he stopped and started to scream. He covered his mouth and backed up. I stood in front of him in the doorway.

About twenty-five feet ahead of me was Susan Newman suspended mid-air, hanging by her neck. The white bed sheet around her neck was tied to the ceiling fan in the living room. It was difficult to tell with her blonde hair in front of her face, but she appeared to have been there for a while. There was a wooden chair to its side underneath her feet. My tunnel vision snapped back when I heard Larry behind me.

"I can't believe this," he said as he backed across the hall.

A few doors down, a woman in her fifties wearing a bathrobe leaned into the hallway. "What's going on?"

"Call the cops!" I yelled.

"Why? What's goin—"

"Now!"

When she could tell it wasn't a prank by Larry's panicking and my serious face, she went back into her apartment and slammed the door.

I grabbed Larry by the shoulders and tried to get him to focus on me. He simultaneously moved his hands in front of his face and shook his head like he was experiencing an acid dream. I shook him a little so I could get him back to the now. After he controlled his shaking, he looked at me. I took in a deep breath and spoke calmly.

"I need you to go back downstairs and wait for the police. If they're not here within ten minutes, I need you to call them. And continue calling until someone shows up. Do you understand me?"

He didn't say anything. All he could do was move his head up and down like the words weren't getting through. I guided him back to the elevator, watching as he got on, and pushed the button for the first floor.

Once the elevator doors shut, I wasted no time quickly heading back into Susan's apartment. I was careful not to touch anything and to keep my distance from her body. I took out my phone and started to take pictures. Before the people in blue showed up and started to tear away the crime scene, I had to record it the way it was so the guys and myself could decipher it. I carefully planted my feet, pointing the camera towards Susan's body.

As I kept taking photos of Susan and the surrounding area, my head couldn't stop reminding me of the two women I had failed to protect. I hadn't had the physical strength to protect Thelma, and then fast forward to a woman whom I had failed because I lacked the mental state to see the bigger picture.

I sent dozens of pictures to both David and Goliath without any context. They would be confused by the photos at first, but it would all be explained later. I wanted to make sure I had copies made, just in case my phone died or was taken away and everything in the rectangular computer was lost forever.

My mind started to fill in different scenarios about what

happened. The first thought was that Susan had been murdered. My theory started to blossom looking at the chair underneath her body. It looked like it was put there as opposed to Susan knocking it over to let the sheet strangle her.

I noticed, when my focus backed away from the chair, that the area itself appeared to be staged. It looked like someone, or some people, had moved the furniture and other objects around to make it seem no one was there. Either Susan had used the time before hanging herself to clean up her apartment or somebody had made sure the cops didn't suspect a thing. This was going to prove difficult later, because I knew the police would say this was suicide and close the case.

But my mind still tortured me with the possibility of suicide. Did I want the scene to look like a murder because I couldn't accept the fact that I was partially responsible? Was my mind trying to create a fake puzzle because the reality was staring me in the face and all I wanted to do was look away? I had to shake that off and let myself view the scene like any other crime scene. I told myself to hold off the depression for later.

The footsteps coming down the hallway made me put my phone back in my pocket. I took a few steps backwards so I was closer to the door. Two police officers in standard uniforms entered the apartment. One was shorter with a crew cut and heavy eyes, while his partner had hair slightly longer and a face that wasn't as intense. Both looked like they had just come from their high-school graduation. The smaller one was the first to speak.

"Were you the other person who discovered the body?" he asked. His voice was deep and formal.

I nodded. "I did. My name is Truman Pierce."

"Why are you still here? I thought you would be downstairs with the building supervisor right now." His tone shifted to detective, but I wasn't buying it.

"I was helping Ms. Newman out with a missing person case. She—"

He pointed to Susan's hanging body. "And that's the name of the deceased?"

"Yes. I was helping her find her sister. I came here when she didn't get back to me."

They both nodded, but I could tell by the way they stared at me that I was a person of interest. Each looked around the room for a few moments before the taller cop radioed in that they needed an ambulance brought to the address. The younger one motioned towards the door.

He said, "Thank you, but you need to go downstairs and wait for backup to show."

I said nothing as I walked out of the apartment and down the hall to the elevator. I wasn't more than fifteen feet away from the apartment when I heard the taller cop speak to his partner.

He said, "He was trying to help her? Didn't do much good."

11

Early morning and I sat in a sturdy chair in front of Longhorn's desk. I wasn't brought in as a suspect. I drove in on my own accord and requested both Detective Longhorn and Detective Johns come in so I can explain to them what happened. I knew both detectives would be banging their fists on my door in due time, so I thought I'd cut right to the chase.

Longhorn sat across from me at his desk, jotting down a couple of notes on a legal pad. He was the first to show and we waited together for his partner to arrive. Longhorn looked at me a few times, glancing up occasionally during his note taking. He wore a dark blue, button-down shirt and khakis—I had seen him wear this same combo multiple times.

Johns walked in a little after eight. Normally, this time of the morning meant he had his shoulders slumped and a pissed-off look across his face, but he walked with purpose as he kept his eyes on me. People tried to say good morning to him, but he walked past them like he hadn't heard anything. When he made it to Longhorn's desk, he spoke up before any of us could.

"Let's go into one of the interrogation rooms," he said as he moved his eyes between his partner and myself.

"He's not under arrest," said Longhorn.

"As much as I would like to arrest him, it's not because of that."

Without saying more, I got up and followed the detectives. Johns led us down the hallway to the end room. The interrogation room was small enough for only a few people. I understood why he picked it: no one could listen to us. There wasn't a giant two-way mirror for the entire department to stand behind. The only thing was the black camera in the upper corner of the room, but the red light was off, indicating the camera wasn't in-use. The only items in the room were a metal desk and three metal chairs. I took the lone chair on one side while the detectives occupied the other two.

"I just got word they picked up someone who's pleading guilty of breaking into Thelma Reilly's house," Johns said, scowling at me, crossing his arms. "He's the big one Truman had described."

I said nothing as we stared at each other.

Longhorn started to get up. "You brought us in here for that news?"

Johns motioned for his partner to sit, but kept his eyes on me. "But I also heard the guy they're bringing in has a broken finger and is clearly roughed up."

Longhorn sat back down and copied Johns' scowl. I knew this was going to happen between the detectives, so I kept my face neutral, internally telling myself not to flinch. There was silence in the room, probably them waiting for me to fill in the blanks, but I wasn't going to say anything until I absolutely had to.

"Anything you want to tell us?" asked Longhorn.

I shrugged.

Johns said, "If you think this is a way for us to arrest you, you're wrong. You're a lot of things, but stupid isn't one of them. You must've visited Stephen for a reason. The officers who arrested him said he's admitting to the crime and that's it. My guess is he's not going to give anyone up or give us anything more than what he's told." He looked at Longhorn, then back at me. "You have my word that we won't arrest you."

Longhorn didn't make any facial expressions that told me Johns was lying. I could do the stupid thing and just sit there with my arms crossed for as long as I could, but I knew there wasn't time to sit around and act like an obnoxious teenager. I was worth more on the outside than in an interrogation room.

I leaned forward and started telling them about what had happened for the past few days. I eased back on the details of what I had physically done to Stephen, but they would soon know about the specifics when they saw his report. I went into how he didn't know anything about Tony, but gave them the name Darren Carver. Johns nodded, while Longhorn looked a little lost without his pen and notepad. I then described Kathleen and my rush to Susan's apartment.

When I was done with everything, the three of us sat in the room for some time. The detectives looked just as confused as me, contemplating. Longhorn was the first to speak.

"And you don't know anything more about Tony?" he asked.

I shook my head.

Longhorn continued, "We'll start looking into this Darren Carver. Hopefully we can get him picked up today." He stood up and started for the door. "I'll also send some patrol officers to Kathleen Newman's place. We might get lucky and she'll be there, but first we'll send out an APB for her and search the area."

Johns and I stayed put, looking at each other after Longhorn left. We had a staring contest as we each tried to figure out what the other was thinking. I had given them everything they needed to know so they could do their jobs and I could do mine. But him sitting there, arms crossed, told me he was ready to tussle some more to get me to spill out every thought. He finally leaned forward, but kept his arms crossed.

"It takes me a long time to finally admit to something I can't control. I want to believe that there are certain things and events in my life that can be controlled, but I know that's not the case—long after things have been settled. You are one of these things. I know now that controlling you will only make you stronger. You jump through every hoop thrown at you, but I know that eventually things will get to you." He uncrossed his arms and spread them like wings. "Just ask any old-timer like myself in this precinct."

I said, "Are you going to arrest me when everything is done, seeing what charges can stick?"

He shook his head. "Only if you're stupid. No, I'm telling you that the weight has already been brought down onto your shoulders, and I'm watching the same experience that has happened to me and several other cops."

"What am I supposed to do?" I asked, rolling my eyes. "Walk away now and let you cops fumble the investigation?"

"And there's the sarcastic mouth I want to punch. You might think Thelma meant more to you than she did to me, but that doesn't mean you have to set fire to everything. I can tell you're someone that didn't have the happy home life growing up."

"Dad was an abusive drunk and mom died when I was young—an original American story."

Johns put his hands on the table. "And Thelma must've been the only person that gave a damn about you. Yeah, very original, but how long until that pain and suffering completely breaks you?"

I started to get up. "If you don't have anything worthwhile to say, then I'm out. Thanks for the pep talk, dad."

He also stood up. "I'm not your father and I would be ashamed to call you my kin."

I paused and turned to Johns. I never thought I would be halted by his words and not by physical force. He didn't have a smirk like he usually gave me after a mental punch, but he wore an angry, disappointed look.

He continued, "Throwing you in one of the jail cells would be the best thing for everybody. You stomp around like an entitled child, thinking the world doesn't understand your pain. If you don't get arrested, then you'll eventually be killed by someone you can't overcome." He folded his arms. "Stop acting like Thelma was the only person in your life. You're dumb to the fact she meant a lot to others, including myself, but you pretend she started existing the second you bummed your way into town. Grow up, child."

I said nothing as I exited the room. The only thing I heard was Johns' disappointed sigh.

Detective Johns had been a lot of things to me up until that point, but for him to calmly dismantle me and act like he cared was a new thing. Most of the time when he talked, he looked as if he wanted to put my head through a wall. The quieter approach he displayed meant he was either ready to give up on me or he knew something I didn't. A smirk on his face was more dangerous to me than any high-frequency insults coming out of his mouth. I didn't know what was worse: him trying to wring my neck or the subtle condescension.

Out front, David and Goliath were waiting for me. We were on the same wavelength as I saw they had also parked their car in the back part of the lot like me. I needed only a few minutes to speak to them, but I didn't want the entire police force listening in on the conversation. The guys understood the situation, keeping close to me and not recklessly shouting out what was on their minds. When I was close enough, Goliath spoke up.

"It's not every day we get multiple pictures sent to us of someone hanging by their neck," he said. "What's going on?"

I looked back at the precinct before I turned and addressed

them. "That was Susan Newman—the one who wanted me to locate her sister."

They each turned slightly as they kept walking.

I continued, "There are multiple things I need both you guys to do. One, I need you to look into the pictures I sent you. Something doesn't add up, but I can't just give hunches and theories to the cops."

David said, "It might look staged, but we'll see if we can find anything."

"While you're looking through them, I need you to find Kathleen Newman. She's been missing for a while, but the picture at Stephen's shack tells me she may still be breathing. Find out everything about her. We need to figure out where she's going or where she would turn at a time like this."

"I'll start looking into it," said David.

I nodded, then looked at Goliath. "You'll need to find someone named Darren Carver." I held up my hand before he could ask the obvious. "He was one of the intruders that night Thelma died. I already told the cops his name, so you'll need to find out about him before they do. He knows where I can find Tony."

Goliath nodded.

David's face turned surprised. "I almost forgot to tell you, but we found information on Edmund Thornton."

I almost told him we had bigger fish to fry, but motioned for him to tell me quickly what he'd found.

He said, "The guy is another asshole dressed in a suit with a fake smile. His company, over the past few years, has been buying up land to put in more modern-day nonsense. Since the market is high right now, he's made a killing ripping people off buying their properties and tripling the land value to prospective buyers. He's monopolizing land throughout town."

Great, I thought. Another rich person who doesn't understand the word no who will make sure my small bank account has been bled dry by dragging me through the system to get the house.

"The problem with him is he's squeaky clean," he continued. "Everything that makes him look like a crook is within the law. He does charity work and has given millions back for public parks, libraries, hospitals, and anything else that will make the public in awe of him."

"Yeah, I get it," I said. "How about his right-hand man?"

"I had to dig a little because your description didn't add up to the name."

"And what's his name?" I asked.

"Chester Watson from Trenton, New Jersey."

I rolled my eyes. "Figures. What did you find on him?"

"Makes sense why Edmund hired him. He did a tour in Afghanistan with the Marines, worked several years in the NYPD, and then went private, making ten times as much doing security for the wealthy. The man is trigger-happy, winning a few marksmanship awards and bragging on social media about the dozens he's killed overseas."

Wonderful, I thought. I was dealing with a person whose credentials were serving his country and then becoming a rodeo clown to the highest bidder. I should've known better than to judge a book by its cover. Moving forward, Edmund would continue to use him to intimidate me, and I wouldn't allow that to back me down. Whenever I saw the two, I would have to turn my backbone into steel.

I said, "All right, I'll worry about the suit and his sidekick. The man has resources, so it wouldn't surprise me if he already knows about you two. If he or anyone from his company tries to contact you, just tell them to get in touch with me."

They both agreed.

"But for now, we need to find Kathleen and Darren. There has to be a pattern, and I hope we find it before they find each other." I looked once more towards the precinct, then back to them. "I'm heading to work, so text me if you come up with anything."

Again, they both said they would.

As I climbed into my car, I had a weird feeling I was being watched, but not by the cops. It felt the same as when you see the outline of something in your peripheral vision, but when you turn, there's nothing there. The person watching could've been a mile away, but the feeling was off. Instead of looking around like a crazy person in a police-station parking lot, I turned the engine over and drove away.

12

I spent most of my time at the college cleaning out the trash bins and mopping the floors. I purposely kept to myself, using the time to move the mop back and forth to give myself the space needed for the mental storm in my head. I wanted to keep up with my schedule and not give Henderson a reason to fire me, but it was difficult when the anvil of information wouldn't let up. I made sure to occasionally check in with Henderson and make it seem like everything was copacetic.

I couldn't stop trying to draw the line through the maze to connect Kathleen Newman to Stephen Williams. Every time I tried to make the connection, I ended up drawing it into a dead end. What did she have or know that would make lowlifes come after her? It bothered me even more that the same people after her had killed Thelma.

Maybe my interest in finding Kathleen was not just the mystery behind why multiple people were looking for her, but to save one person after I'd failed the others. My grip tightened along the mop handle when I pictured Thelma's and Susan's deceased faces. I wanted to think anyone would feel protected with me, but I knew that wasn't the case. I couldn't handle another dead body that I could've prevented.

The thoughts swirling in my head were causing me to be an

antisocial old man. Professors and students who tried to stop and chat with me were met with a cold shoulder and a don't-bother-me attitude. I knew what I was doing and how it looked, but I didn't feel like making new friends. I was putting up a force field, making sure I hurt no one else.

I had a few hours left on my shift, keeping my eyes down on the mop I was pushing around in the hallway, when two pairs of legs walked up to me. Thinking they were students, I kept my eyes to the floor to make sure they understood to keep walking. But they didn't. Instead, the legs stood there like statues. When I looked at them, the first thing I noticed was the expensive dark slacks one pair of legs wore. My eyes looked up and found Edmund and Chester. The judging looks on their faces seemed like they wanted to say something, but I wasn't going to be the first to speak. Finally, Chester spoke.

"The man just inherited some money and here he is pushing around a mop," he said with a smirk. "Perfect."

"It's good to see you again, Chester."

His smirk disappeared. "How did you...my name is Tex."

"Whatever you say, Chester."

He took a step towards me, but Edmund grabbed his arm. Even though someone Chester's size should've dragged Edmund, Chester stopped like he was turned into stone and didn't budge. Not only his body stop moving, but also his face changed from annoyance to calm in seconds. Edmund did a good job keeping his pet under control.

"Mr. Pierce," Edmund said with a smile, "we came here to have a talk with you about the other day. I understand things were emotional the last time we saw each other. It was a bit of a shock for all parties involved."

"That's one way of putting it," I said.

He ignored that. "I'm here today to talk to you about clearing the air and pushing aside our differences."

"And what would that be?"

He looked around. "Is there a conference room or office where we can speak privately?"

There was nothing I wanted more than to tell them off, and then personally throw them out of the building. From their determined looks, I knew this was a futile move. They looked like they would keep coming back until they said what was spinning in their heads. I sighed, motioning down the hallway towards the conference rooms.

I said, "You have a few minutes, and then you're gone."

"I don't think anyone would mind my class wandering the facilities," he replied.

I rolled my eyes but didn't say anything as I moved the mop and bucket against the wall. I led them down the hall, listening to them quietly converse between themselves like a couple of high schoolers. They were mostly mumbling, but I figured they wanted to keep trash talking about me and my employment world.

Out of the three conference rooms, one was being used by a group of students, but the other two were empty. The room I took them to had white walls, brown-carpeted flooring, and a long, brown table with a dozen cushioned chairs surrounding it. I motioned for them to sit at one end of the table while I took my place at the other end. I wanted as much space between us as possible. Neither objected as Edmund took the end seat and Chester took a seat next to him on the corner like a child. Before I sat down, I took my phone out of my pocket and laid it on the table.

"Mr. Pierce," said Edmund, crossing one arm over the other on the tabletop, "like I said before, I know that things between us have gotten off to a rocky start, but I want to change that today. No one wants to see any more animosity."

"And what makes you think I want any changes right now?" I asked.

He smiled. "Who wouldn't want a little fortune sent their way?"

I sighed. "Fine, I'll bite. What do you have in mind?"

"Well," he said, easing back in the chair, "my aunt's place wasn't worth much. It—"

"It was worth more than you realize."

"Maybe in memories, but that doesn't mean anything in the real-estate world. Right now, the market is high and people are paying good money for land. The house is pretty much worthless—except for those precious memories you have stored. The land is worth much more. I am here today to make a deal with you for the lot."

"I don't care if it was made of solid gold, you're not getting it."

Edmund grinned like he'd expected my statement. "What I'm trying to do today, Mr. Pierce, is give you my respect before the system comes in and things go my way. Now, I don't want to be that type of person, but you aren't the first to go against me in this manner."

Edmund continued his unoriginal and clichéd threats, and my eyes occasionally glanced over at Chester. He sat with his arms crossed like he was praying the civilized discussions would fall through and he would have to enact his plan of action. He hadn't used physical force yet, but my experiences always taught me to be wary of the quiet ones.

"So," Edmund said, "what I am offering you today is a million dollars—no strings attached. I'm basing this off of the fact that my aunt gave you half-a-million dollars with the house and lot. That amount means little to me." He squared his shoulders. "I can have the money to you by the end of the day."

"And what do you plan on doing with that land after you tear down the house?"

"My goal is to start building parking garages in that particular area. A shopping center is being planned right down the street, and I want to make sure I get the land for parking areas now before it becoming a problem later."

"So, you're not using the land for affordable housing or anything helpful to give back to the community?"

He shrugged. "I'm giving them parking garages."

"And I can see where you get your humanity awards from."

My phone started lighting up like a Christmas tree. David was throwing text after text at me. I half looked down as Edmund talked and Chester sulked. At first, David was giving me general information he had found about Kathleen Newman, like her birthday, address, and any other information I could make out before another text showed. I made sure not to stare at my phone like everyone else, but my curiosity wanted to know if David had found anything useful. Edmund didn't seem to mind, but Chester looked annoyed.

Edmund said, "Mr. Pierce, I don't want to resort to other methods to acquire the property."

This snapped me back. "Are you threatening me?"

"I'm giving you the world we live in, Mr. Pierce. You can see that a number of your neighbors have wisely sold their properties. I have ways of forcing people to be on the same page as me."

I pointed at Chester. "And does that mean a visit from your puppet?"

Chester leaned forward. "I'm no one's pet, Janitor."

"How original."

"Gentlemen, please," said Edmund. "What I mean is using the

law to my advantage. There are enough politicians and judges who will understand my point of view and take my side."

I shook my head, looking down towards the table while the spoiled child kept talking. I knew another sarcastic remark was only going to be blocked with one of his tough-man comments. I could tell Edmund would keep harassing me until I told him with a smile that he could have the house, the land, my respect, and the shirt off my back.

While he kept talking, my phone blazed with another text from David. I was getting tired of the rectangular glow, but chose the machine over Edmund's nails-to-the-chalkboard voice. I didn't have to move my face close to the cell because David wrote the message out in all caps.

KATHLEEN WORKED AT THORNTON CONSTRUCTION!!!!!

I kept my poker face as I glanced at Edmund and Chester. One continued to give me the business proposition from hell while the other scowled at me like a trained dog. I didn't think they could pick up my sudden change. Neither of them made any move to show they understood my internal shock.

What did Kathleen have to do with Edmund's business? A thousand questions started to populate my mind. Did the two in front of me have anything to do with her disappearance? Where did the construction company fit into the equation? Did Kathleen have something on anyone in the company that had either put her on the run or made her disappear, like Jimmy Hoffa, from the company? Or was it all a big coincidence?

For a split second, I asked myself if I should stop talking about the money and the land and start asking them about Kathleen, but

I quickly put that to bed. These two didn't seem like the type for a guy like me to start asking questions about a missing woman. First, I needed something that I could use to pin them to Kathleen—if that was the case.

Or maybe I was using Kathleen's disappearance as a way to get them off my back about the house and land. I could've accused them at that moment, but chances are they would've laughed like I had just told a childish joke. If they did take me seriously, then how far would I get before I ended up missing like Kathleen?

There was only own way I could handle the situation.

"You know," I said, "your proposal doesn't sound too bad. Let me take some time to think it over."

Edmund stopped midsentence and gave me a hopeful look. Chester raised his eyebrows in the same surprise.

"Really?" Edmund asked. "You seemed pretty adamant a moment ago."

I shrugged. "There are still a lot of emotions pumping through me. It's best if we take a little more time with this. I know you're eager to get the land, but I want to make sure everything is straight when I do."

"That seems reasonable." He said that like his mind was still wrapping around the idea. "Please get in touch with my secretary when you want to make the right decision."

Without waiting for my response, both got up and started to exit the room. It was difficult to tell from their poker faces whether they believed me or not, but it was enough to get them to leave. Chances were good that they were going to rehash the conversation later, but there was nothing more I could do to add to or subtract from the theories flying through their heads.

I walked them out into the hallway like I was a gracious host and pointed towards the exit. They said their goodbyes. I found it strange from Chester because I thought he was going to tell me to pick up garbage or give me another mindless command, but he tipped his cowboy hat at me like I was a long-lost friend. I mentally shook it off as I went back into the conference room and locked the door. I hit David's number after giving a quick glance out the door's window.

"I saw your text," I said. "What's going on?" I didn't want to waste time.

David said, "It's by luck we found her employment. Goliath searched her social media and found a post about it. We did a check through the company's registry and her name popped up. As far as we know, she is still employed there, but there's not much listed about her."

"Doesn't sound promising at all. I'm surprised they didn't completely scrub her name. Did you look into her current whereabouts?"

Goliath piped up in the background. "I was able to pull up her latest credit card purchases. Kathleen, or someone using her card, stayed at a motel on the outskirts of town a few days ago."

"And she hasn't used her card, or any other card, since?"

"Just to take out some cash from an ATM near the motel. She withdrew it the same day she checked into the motel. Chances are she's moved on."

"That's why I'll go after work to see what I can find. It seems like someone either stole her card or she's moving around a lot. Whatever the reason, I need to get a better answer than just guessing."

I told them to keep me updated if they found anything more, and then hung up.

There were parts of me that wanted to run out of the building and search for Kathleen, but I didn't want to run into something without the full story; that could only lead to trouble. I talked to David and Goliath like she was still alive because her credit card was still active, but that didn't mean the person using it was her. That was a good ploy from a kidnapper or murderer to throw us off the track. I was looking for a phantom with a possible stolen credit card.

But the other big reason why I wanted things to stew was learning that Kathleen had worked at Edmund's company. Just when I'd thought I understood the situation, life threw me another curveball.

I went back to the rest of my shift, but made it a bigger point to be antisocial with everyone. I turned on my mental cruise control. All I could do with my brain was plan out the next course of action. There were several pieces of a puzzle getting dumped on me that I'd never asked for.

At the end of my shift, I said my usual goodbye to Henderson, letting him know I would see him soon. He gave me an approval nod like he was surprised to see me actually finish my shift and leave work on time. I finally walked out, but with a head full of theories and mazes.

I was walking straight into the abyss.

13

I drove to the outskirts based on the address the guys had given to me. It was no surprise when I pulled up to the motel that it should have been repaired decades ago. The two-story motel was covered in what used to be sky blue but had now turned into a sludge-like faded color. There was graffiti on both ends of the motel, but from the obvious leftover markings it looked like someone had tried to wash the middle part.

I parked in a spot near the front office at the right corner. When I got out, there were a few kids riding by in bikes, giving me the stink eye. I ignored them, assuming my car would have new decorations of dents and piss smell if I provoked them. As I walked towards the front office, I kept most of my senses hidden inside, observing the kids pedaling around the corner.

The office was worse than the building's exterior. As I stepped inside, the smell of cigarettes and stale donuts thumped me. The linoleum flooring looked like someone forgot to run a broom for the past twenty years. A pimply-faced man in either his late teens or early twenties sat at the front counter, feet up and back leaning into a seat with a torn cushion. He hadn't noticed me walking up until I gave two knocks on the dusty counter.

"Uh, yes," he said, putting his feet on the floor. "How can I help you?"

I took out a picture of Kathleen and held it close to him. "I want to know if this woman has passed through here in the past couple of days."

He gave me a quizzical look. "Are you a cop?"

"Not a cop. She's gone missing and I've been hired to find her." He didn't need the play-by-play story.

"Missing? She didn't seem in distress when she was here."

"And when was that?"

"Two days ago." He pointed towards the rooms. "She stayed in Room 7."

"Is anyone currently staying there?"

He shook his head.

"I need a key to check out Room 7 for a few minutes." I took out my wallet. "I'll pay for a day's stay."

He shrugged his shoulders, then proceeded to ring me up for the room. This was one of the few places in the country where you could pay cash. After he handed me a receipt, he slid the electronic key over to me. For some reason, I thought he was going to give me a copper key with a plastic diamond attached. I took the key without question and went to the room.

At first, the key wouldn't work for the door. I inserted it a few times, only to get a red light blinking and the door handle unmoved. I was getting upset, thinking of marching back into the office and asking why the key card was defective. I tried once more and the green light finally appeared. The handle moved and I slowly pushed the door open.

I didn't get more than a few inches when something pushed my head into the door with force and sent me flying into the room. My body landed on the brown-carpeted floor, but my head was seeing four of everything.

How could I be so stupid? I internally repeated while trying not to pass out.

I turned over slowly, and in the doorway was the outline of a man with the sun behind him. He walked up to me. I would've made him already, but my vision was going in and out. The person kneeled down next to me, moving in front of my peripheral. Just before I passed out, I saw one brown pupil and one green. I wanted to say Crazy Eyes, but I blacked out.

"Hey, mister!"

I slowly opened my eyes to find three teens standing right outside the motel room. Everything was double vision, but I could still see each had their hands on bicycle handles. They matched, wearing jeans and dark, long-sleeved shirts in different colors. The teen in the middle was motioning to me.

"I said, 'Hey, mister!'" he repeated.

I knew where I was and what had ensued, but I was still getting my senses back so I could speak with clarity. I lifted my body but still sat on the floor. When my head stopped spinning just enough, all I could envision were the different-color pupils.

"Where did the man go that was in here?" I asked while rubbing my head.

The one on the left with long blond hair pointed towards the road. "He ran off when we saw what he did to you. We started screaming at him and he ran off."

I stood up and shook my head a few times as I walked outside. The teens moved out of the way as I scanned the area. The blurriness was slowly dissipating and I was steadily feeling better. I was going to ask the teens where Darren ran off to, but I knew he was already long gone. I used the next minute to collect myself before speaking. I took out my wallet and gave each teen a twenty.

"Thanks for the help," I said to them.

They each took their bill and pedaled away.

I went back to the front office and slammed the key card on top of the counter without saying a word to the clerk. He went to say something, but I was out the door before we could have any conversation.

Furious was an understatement. I couldn't believe one of those thieves got the drop on me again. My blurred vision turned to red. Instead of dizziness, my head was now filled with me bashing their heads through glass windows. The humiliation I felt for not being able to do a better job with my surroundings was burning a hole through me. I'd thought I was dealing with amateurs like Stephen, but it was clear now that they weren't.

I got into my car and peeled out of the parking lot, leaving a trail of smoke. I took my phone out of my pocket and put it on speaker as I hit David's number. I tossed the phone on the passenger seat and waited for a voice. When the phone was answered, I started talking before he could get a word in.

"I need the both of you to come to my place as soon as possible." He started to speak, but I cut him off. "Get me all the information you have on Kathleen. More specifically, I need all the areas where she's used her credit card since she's been missing."

I reached over and pressed End on the phone.

My mind wouldn't leave the motel scene. I had to see past the anger for Darren because I had to know what he knew and fill in certain blanks. How long had he been following me? Was he even following me or was it a big coincidence and he had happened to be in the same area looking for Kathleen?

When I got home, I went through the walkout basement and sat down at the kitchen table. Later, it would occur to me: that had been the first time I hadn't anticipated anyone would be waiting at my place to attack me. By then, I'd had enough of the surprises and bullshit. My head had a flaring migraine, so I just sat there with the lights dimmed, waiting for David and Goliath to show.

Over thirty minutes passed before the guys arrived. I hadn't moved from my spot when they walked through the door without knocking. They saw me sitting with a stern look on my face and they knew not to lead with any chitchat. They took chairs and put their laptops and phones on the table. They wasted no time in explaining the situation.

David said, "We put pins on every location Kathleen has been since she was reported missing." He opened the laptop and the screen lit up. "I didn't notice until we put the pins on each place that she had been using the card."

He didn't say anything more as he typed on the keyboard. After punching in some letters and numbers, he turned the screen towards me. It was clear the moment I saw the screen. On the glowing rectangle were a number of red and blue pins that formed a circle throughout town—mostly on the outskirts. I already knew what was going on, but David went ahead.

"She's going in a circle," he said. "The red pins are places that she went to first, and the blue pins represent the same places she went to a second time. She, or whoever has her card, is moving around every couple of days."

David kept talking, but I was mentally looking for more patterns. My eyes started from the top and went in a clocklike direction to study the path. I stopped at the top-left corner. There were a number of red pins in the area but few blue pins. I checked to see if there were gaps in any other places, but came up with inconsistency.

"This is the area where I'll start," I said, pointing to the top-left corner.

David and Goliath both looked at the screen.

Goliath said, "That's a good place to start. If there's anything we can learn from this, it's that she, or whoever it is, hasn't completed the second circle yet. I'm not entirely sure, though."

"What do you mean?" I asked.

"Well, and let's assume it's her, she can't keep running forever. Maybe she doesn't want to be found. Or worse, if we can find this pattern, then there are others who will be able to put the puzzle together, too."

"It looks like you might be right."

"What do you mean?" he asked.

"Darren Carver got the jump on me at the motel."

Both paused.

I continued, "Neither of us found her, but he's out there right now looking for her." I sighed, disappointed. "I don't understand why the cops haven't picked him up yet."

"I've been trying to find him," said Goliath, "but he's jumping around fast. Several times the cops have gone to his place, but no luck."

"Don't try to be tough and apprehend him if you see him," I said. "He's not as dumb as Stephen. He's made it clear he can move around, and chances are he's keeping tabs on me right now, so assume he knows about the two of you." I got up and moved a few steps. "Find out what you can about Darren and see if you can track him down. Let me know if you have something."

"Where are you going?" asked David.

I pointed to the map. "I'm starting with the motels that she hasn't been to a second time. Now that I have an idea where she is going, I can go through town like I know what I'm doing. I'm going to need addr—"

My phone buzzed. It was a text message with a list of motel addresses. I looked up just as Goliath put his phone away, grinning at me.

“Now let’s see if you can pull the same magic with Darren,” I said.

Before I could say anything else, both guys had their heads planted in their electronic devices, looking for leads. A few years ago, I would’ve laughed at the sight. Now the sight was a show of hope.

14

I was driving to the second motel on the list Goliath had texted me, already feeling disgruntled by the lack of progress I'd made. The first motel I went to I'd known would be a bust by how deserted the parking lot appeared. When I tried to talk to the stoned-out clerk, he mumbled that there hadn't been anyone checked in for the past few days. I even waited in my car for about a minute, frustrated, before going to the next address.

When I pulled up to the second motel, the first thing I noticed were the few cars in the parking lot, so I hung back across the street and scoped out the place for a short time. I wasn't in any hurry to run through the parking lot to ask the desk clerk if their hazy memory remembered Kathleen. Also, I wanted some to time to scope out my surroundings and to check if Darren—or anyone—was following me.

The two-story structure appeared to be newer than the others I'd been seeing for the past few days. It looked as if the person or persons running the place actually cared about making money and what people thought. The blue and green paint on the exterior walls looked to be relatively new and the stairs leading up to the second level seemed to have been put in during the last few years.

While waiting, I took my phone out several times, thinking of calling Henderson and just quitting on the spot. I had been missing work a lot lately, but that was before finding the yellow brick road to Kathleen. Henderson wasn't going to accept more excuses, and it felt like I had to cut the final piece of string holding me up. In the end, I put the phone away for good because I didn't know where things with Kathleen would go and it was better to have employment at the moment than to drop everything over speculation.

After a few minutes more, I decided I didn't want to look like a creep sitting alone in a car, so I got out and walked a couple of blocks down the street to a convenience store. This helped put my mind at ease: if anyone was following me, I could get the jump on them first. When I walked in, I went all the way to the back where the refrigerated drinks were kept. I pretended to browse the selection, but used the opportunity to focus on the front of the store. Luckily the store only had a few people scattered around, making it easier for me to scout the front. It was around the time when the store clerk started to ask me if I was going to buy anything that I exited the facility, feeling the peace of mind I needed.

On my way back to the motel, I started to cross the street and make my way to the main office to have a chat with the clerk when I saw Kathleen Newman step out from Room 27 on the second level. Even from a distance, I could tell it was her by the pictures I had seen. Her hair seemed blonder than any picture I'd seen. She wore a red T-shirt and jean shorts that showed off her tan skin. I stood in place, watching as she only took a few steps out before patting her pockets, and then going back into her room.

I walked up the stairs. I didn't make any big sounds, but it wasn't like I'd thought she could hear me. I acted casual, making sure no one, especially Kathleen, would think I didn't belong there. My legs walked like I'd paid for a room and was trying to find the correct door number.

I walked up to Room 27, made a fist, ready to knock, but I

stopped myself. It was then that I realized I hadn't thought everything through that could happen. Did Kathleen know about me? Was she aware of her sister's fate? If I knocked, would she have a gun, ready to shoot, and then run off? You never know how far a person will take it when they are on the run. In the end, I didn't have the time to make small decisions when the woman behind the door had a target on her back like me.

Not more than a few seconds after I had knocked on the door, I heard feet shuffling. I turned my head to get a better listen. She didn't ask who was there or make any other sounds than her footfall. It went quiet for a few seconds, then I heard noises again. I stood still, not making any movements to indicate I was ready to use force to break down the door and drag her out. Places like this motel normally don't have windows in the back of the room, so the only way out was through the door or the window directly next to it. It had felt like I was standing out there for days until I heard a voice from the other side speak up.

"Yes," she said, clearing her throat. "Who is it?" She did her best to act casual, but bubbles of hesitation floated to the top.

Calmly, I said, "My name is Truman Pierce, Kathleen. I was sent by your sister, Susan, to find you."

No answer.

"I have been searching for you for a while and it's important that we talk. This has to do with what you're into. I want to make it clear that I don't work for Edmund Thornton."

No answer.

I inhaled. "There are things that I must discuss with you in private and not from out here." I lowered my voice some. "Something happened to your sister."

The door opened slightly. A brass chain stopped the door after a few inches. Kathleen opened it enough that I could see her tanned skin and blue eyes looking directly at me. Her face was dour, trying to detect in that silent moment whether or not I was telling the truth.

"Let me see your driver's license," she demanded.

Slowly, I took out my wallet so I didn't spook her and removed my driver's license from the pocket. I moved the polycarbonate rectangle enough so she could see without intruding into her space. She studied the license for a few seconds, even squinting at it. Finally, she closed the door on me and I used that moment to put the license in my pocket while I heard her remove the chain. When she opened the door, she stood a few feet from me. I didn't assume I should start moving into the room.

"I've heard about you from online articles," Kathleen said. "That's the only reason why I opened the door."

"May I come in?" I asked.

Once again, she took a moment to quietly consider her options. She crossed her arms like an unnerved parent, but I kept my distance and treated the doorframe like it was a shield that couldn't be crossed. I knew I was in when she lowered her arms and the muscles in her face relaxed.

"Hurry," she said. "And close the door."

I did as she said. There was a circular wooden table to my left with only one chair. An unmade bed with clothes and papers scattered around like snow. A bedside table with more papers scattered all over also held a lamp sitting close to the edge. She might've only occupied the room for a few days, but Kathleen treated the space as if she had been permanently living there for years.

Kathleen sat on the bed, trying her best not to crumple the papers. I wouldn't move until she trusted me enough to say it was fine to sit down. She didn't. Instead, she looked at me like we were in the middle of a game of don't blink. After a minute, I was ready to say something, but she spoke first.

"So," she said, "my sister sent you for me?"

I nodded. I readied myself to give her the bad news, since her tone made it seem like Susan was still alive. "About your sister. She..." It was difficult to get out.

"Yes?" she asked with a puzzled look.

"Kathleen, I'm sorry to tell you, but your sister has passed."

Her face went from puzzled to shocked. "Passed?"

"She died. One of the reasons why I've looked for you is to see if you were okay."

"How?"

I inhaled. "Her body was found hanged in her apartment."

The extra gravity in the room hit Kathleen. She got up from the bed, letting pieces of discarded clothing hit the ground. She dragged her feet around the carpeting like it was her first time there. Her eyes ran up the wall and looked across the ceiling like there was a line only she could make out. When she was ready, she turned in my direction. Her eyes seemed to be looking right through me.

"No," she finally said, "that doesn't make any sense. Susan wasn't suicidal. She never had those types of thoughts before. At least, she never told me she did nor showed any signs."

"I'm just letting you know what I saw with my own eyes."

I could tell she wanted nothing more than to cry right there, but she held back the tears. She lost all color in her face and her arms went limp. She opened her mouth to say something, but quickly closed it. After a minute, she started to speak as she walked to the door.

"Thanks for the message," she said, "but you can go on your way now."

I didn't move. "Another reason why I'm here is to convince

you to come with me." I held up a hand when she started to speak. "I don't know what you've gotten yourself into, but the results are tied into the death of my landlord."

Her face twitched a little. "What are you talking about?"

I motioned to the scattered papers. "You're not going to build a fort out of the papers you took. You have information about Edmund Thornton and the company he runs. Thelma, my landlord, was gunned down, and this coincides with your ties to the same company that wanted to buy her land. This is more than just coincidence."

"And I'm just supposed to tell you everything that happened?" she asked with an annoyed tone and arms crossed.

I nodded. "Yes, that's what you're going to do. You already have a sense of who I am, don't you?"

"I've read about you."

"Then you know what I'm telling you is serious." I sat in a chair, slowly easing back onto the seat's thin cushion. "How did all this begin? Where did you get this information?"

Kathleen surveyed the scattered papers, appearing to gather her thoughts. Every few seconds she took a deep breath, as if she was surprised to be in the middle of a motel room with a stranger. Finally, she sat back down in the same spot on the bed, collecting as many pieces of paper as she could gather within arm's reach. She took the unorganized handfuls and laid them on her lap.

She said, "I'd been working at Mr. Thornton's company for roughly two years. I started off with a good-salary gig and every intention of working up the ladder. Edmund Thornton doesn't have a mega office like you see on TV, but he does have a suitable work area where there's enough people to keep putting money in his pockets. I was a workaholic and everyone in the office knew that about me early on. I was the employee who stayed late at every opportunity and tried to find extra tasks."

I leaned forward as she took in another deep breath.

She continued, "A few months ago, I was running through the numbers and started to see extra accounts that were unnamed with money being sent to them. I'm not sure how these even popped up in the accounts, but I became suspicious." She held up the papers like a flashlight. "I printed them out, but a lot of these were mostly gibberish, nothing I could use to prove any wrongdoing, but I kept digging."

"I was afraid to look like I was snooping, so I usually did it in the evenings when everyone was gone. Little by little things started showing up for me. I could see money being transferred to parties outside of the company and being put into the hands of codenames, such as X or Z—not exactly the most original. The problem was that most of the files were encrypted and I didn't have the skills to break through."

I said, "I know a couple of guys that can assist you, if you got the files."

She ignored me. "So, one day I overheard Mr. Watson jokingly brag to a few people about buying city hall. I thought it was odd and precise, so I went back in once more and found a file named Stevens, as in Councilman Stevens. It was a transaction of fifty-thousand dollars to him directly."

"The next night, after everyone was gone, I printed out all the unencrypted files I could, and then I downloaded both the unencrypted and the encrypted files onto a thumb drive. My goal was to figure out how to break the files' code and send them out to every news website and station. I knew it was a gamble because I had stolen the files, but I also knew that there's more going on than just bribery."

And it *was* a gamble. I knew this whole mess was more than a coincidence, but I was afraid the encrypted files might be useless. If they were, then we were going to have more than just egg on our faces. But given her story and recent events, I also believed we would find embezzlement, fraud, and murder.

"Where's the thumb drive?" I asked.

She was hesitant at first, but then said, "In my purse, on top of the bureau." She motioned towards an oak bureau next to the bathroom door.

"Kathleen, if I could find you, then the people you took the files from aren't far behind. You don't know all the information, but there are people out there who are willing to kill at the drop of a hat just to reclaim the papers and thumb drive. There are two tech wizards who can start decrypting the files. What I can do is help you, but you have to guarantee to me that if we can't find anything on the files, then we'll both have to go to the authorities with what we know and plead guilty to theft." I put my hand on my chest. "That's if you'll agree to the terms."

After pondering for a minute, she agreed.

"Let's collect all your stuff and we'll head over to the guys' place," I said.

It took about fifteen minutes to collect all her possessions and get them into her bags. You could tell with all the junk she carried that if was her first time on the run. I tried to tell her there were things she could throw out, but she insisted everything was a necessity.

I grabbed most of her bags and followed her to the front desk to check out. It would've been faster for me to head straight to the car while she checked out, but I wasn't going to let her out of my sights just so someone could grab her. She looked forward as I scanned my peripherals, not letting anyone get the jump on us.

Once she was checked out, I put her stuff in the trunk of

my car while she got into the passenger seat. Behind the steering wheel, I adjusted the rearview mirror to see if anyone was behind me, and in that moment, I thought I spotted Darren. I turned my head to see with my own two eyes if it was him or an apparition. I didn't see anyone there besides an elderly woman walking out of a convenience store.

"Is there a problem?" Kathleen asked.

I turned forward. Either he was there or not, but I didn't have time to just sit around and wonder what was real. My focus was on Kathleen and not letting anyone do any harm to her. A good night's sleep could cure me of supposed visions I was having, but I had to table that for later. I just lightly shook my head to answer her question.

I started the car and drove to David and Goliath's.

15

When I got Kathleen to the guys' apartment, both acted as if they had been expecting her for over a month. There were few formalities; everyone understood why she was there and no one wasted any time. I closed the blinds as Kathleen took out the thumb drive from her purse and handed it to Goliath. We left most of Kathleen's luggage in the car, but I did my part by bringing up the things she needed the most.

Goliath took no more than a minute looking through the encrypted files before his face went from skeptical to surprised.

"For a construction company, they really know how to keep their security tight," he said. "These files basically have security that goes miles deep. I'm not going to crack this anytime soon. We're lucky to have the papers and files they didn't encrypt, for whatever reason, but we'll take it."

It was the news I had expected, but I was still disappointed. Everyone else showed their equal frustration as they pulled up chairs to sit near Goliath.

Instead of feeling like a lost shoe while listening to Goliath's technical support jargon that would have sailed over my head, I told everyone I was running out and grabbing food since it appeared they weren't planning on getting sleep for the foreseeable future. They kept staring at their computer screens, giving me a half acknowledgement.

In the hallway, I closed the door, and just as I turned to walk down the stairs, Detective Johns stood at the top, arms crossed. He was dressed in his usual tough-guy attire while on the job, including a blazer over a button-down shirt with no tie. The slacks he chose had several wrinkles, but he stood tall, trying his best not to care about other people's opinions. I put on a poker face and pretended like I knew why he was waiting on the second floor of a Chinese restaurant.

He said, "Follow me. We need to talk."

"Am I under arrest?"

"You're not, but I'll put the 'cuffs on you if you start giving me trouble." He uncrossed his arms. "There's a diner a few blocks away where we can talk."

"After you, Detective."

Even though I had been outside thirty minutes earlier, the weather seemed too dreary and gray compared to the sunny reception area. The clouds rolled in, casting a shadow over the streets and buildings, not letting any sunlight through. It seemed as if dusk was only a few minutes away. There weren't any thunder noises or visible signs it was going to rain, but the scenery looked as if it were pulled out of an Edgar Allan Poe story.

Johns and I didn't say anything on the walk over to our destination. He made sure to be a few feet in front of me at all times. Not once did he turn back to see if I was still there, nor did he make any attempt to slow down. He bumped into a few people without apologizing or acting like they existed. I just watched him act like a tough guy and knew why certain things in his life hadn't worked out.

He took me to a small diner five blocks away from the apartment called Lucy's. The exterior had worn white bricks, but it looked like they still had decent business. When we walked inside, a woman in her mid-forties behind the counter recognized Johns and said that he could take his usual spot in the back. There was a row of booths on the right-hand side, and we walked all the way back until we took the last booth. Johns quickly took the side where his back was pointed towards the exit, while I sat on the opposite side. There were a few pictures on the wall that looked to be store-bought. Our table was a bit shaky, but I didn't think we would be there for long.

I said, "So, why did you—"

Johns held up a hand and turned to the woman at the counter. "Marie, we'll just have water. I'm not getting the usual."

Marie nodded, then turned around.

"Is this where you take everyone for one last meal before they eat sludge for life at the prison?" I sarcastically asked.

"This is where I take informants and other people I want to show that I'm serious about what I have to say." He rested his hands on the table. "Or we can pretend it's the nineteen fifties and I'll buy you a pack of cigarettes, but your pathetic generation bitches about that—among other things."

"Yeah, how dare we try to lead healthy lives."

Marie came over with two glasses of room-temperature water and sat them down in front of us. She once again asked Johns if he wanted his usual, but he shook his head. Marie shrugged and walked away to attend to a couple who strolled in.

"So," I said, "is this your way of telling me I need to stop looking for Thelma's killer or are you giving me a warning not to look into a certain case?"

"Why are you going for your PI license?" he asked.

This question caught me off guard. Not only was I giving him every chance to hit me, but he was actively being cool with every insult I threw at him. There was clearly a lot on his mind, and it didn't occur to me then that he was facing a lot of moral discrepancies. I could tell that this conversation must've been going through his head for a while now. I decided to go along with it and actually started conversing with him.

"Because I know I have it in me to get some justice done around here," I replied. "I might not carry a badge and gun like you, but that doesn't mean my only option is to sit on the sidelines and wait for other people to clean up the mess."

He smirked. "That's better than the answer I gave when I was at the academy. It's hard to think of myself as a rookie, but I still remember how I was just gung-ho about being a cop. I wanted to kick ass and push the envelope as much as I could. Sure, I thought I could help people, but I was more interested in how people would look at me, how they could finally say they were proud. I lied to people about wanting to be a public servant and protect them, but I mostly did that because I thought it was the expressway of getting laid. I look back at that young punk I was and wish I could smack him across the head."

Neither of us said anything, letting what he said hover there for a minute. The way he looked at his hands and the slow breaths he took made me realize he had been planning on saying that for a while, and chances are I was the first person he had told. I decided I would wait to say something to him, because I knew he would have more to say. When he was ready to talk more, he waved a hand in front of his face like there was a fly hovering in front of him.

Johns said, "Yeah, so, anyway, Longhorn doesn't know I'm here."

I said nothing.

"No sarcastic comment?"

I shook my head. "No, that ship sailed a minute ago. I have a feeling, for once, that me and you are on the same page."

"That might be the case. Anyway, Longhorn doesn't know I'm here and I want to make sure that neither he nor anyone else at the precinct knows what I'm about to tell you next."

I leaned in a little closer like he was going to whisper.

"The reality is that the department has gotten lost on how to catch Thelma's killer. The only clues we found so far were a direct result of you. Yes, the department has had one of our toughest years, but we act like this case is a never-ending maze."

"And what has Stephen told you?" I asked.

He snorted. "Only what he already told you. He's had more visits from the custodian cleaning up his piss than all the cops who interrogated him combined. By the way, we're still looking into this Darren Carver fella. His residence has had frequent visits from one of my own, but to no avail."

"That's because he's stalking me," I said with irritation.

His face looked like it aged ten years in two seconds. "Excuse me?"

I took a swig of water. "Darren knows I'm going down the right path, so he's been tailing me every chance he gets. He even sent me a message recently by knocking my head through a door."

"And when were you going to tell me about this?"

"I'm still getting over the fact that you and me are becoming temporary partners. Wasn't exactly on my bingo card for the year."

Johns took a swig, and then leaned back. He turned his face and swept the panoramic view of the diner, as if he was taking surveillance of the establishment. He snorted a few times, making sure he got the message through that he wasn't thrilled about what I had just confessed. Or, he was annoyed I was already several steps ahead of him. He turned back to me.

"I guess we're not going to be sharing every detail anytime

soon," he said.

"I'm not the sensitive type, and I need you to show me that I can actually share information without you throwing a hissy fit and threatening to drag me to jail."

He lowered his head and scratched the top enough that I thought he was going to dig all the way to his brain. "I should've taken more of those therapy sessions."

I smiled. "It seems like Thelma was the therapy we didn't realize we had until she was gone."

He nodded. "In times like these, when I started to get angry, I saw Thelma telling me to breathe and not let all the noise of the world get to me."

"She could see the good in everyone and bring it out."

"Once, in high school," Johns said, "I was bullying a kid half my size. I had just started my freshmen year and I wanted to prove that I was the top dog. His name was Freddy and this happened after school. I was doing my best to impress the seniors as a big group hung out in front of a record store, but they weren't buying it. Then I saw Freddy walking down the street, carrying a stack of books. This couldn't have come at a better time. I stuck my foot out and tripped him. He fell on his face as his books went all over the place. Everyone laughed. For that brief moment I felt like the coolest person in the world, like I was invincible."

"But then Mrs. Reilly came marching down the sidewalk from the Laundromat, yelling at me to not move. I had never seen a group of high schoolers more frightened. Several of them scattered, leaving me with Freddy and a few others. I had my head down and did everything I could not to piss myself. When Thelma came up to me, she told me how I should be ashamed of myself. To this day, no one could use words to cut deeper than that woman. She made me clean up Freddy and his books. I didn't just apologize; I also made sure that he didn't have to be afraid of me ever again."

Johns looked to his side with a scowl. He disappeared into his train of thought for a few seconds, and I didn't want to interrupt him. He was more than willing to talk when it came to Thelma.

He said, "Since then, I guess you can say that whenever I feel like my temper is flaring, I can mentally see Mrs. Reilly telling me to cool down." He looked at me. "There are times where I wanted to pop your head like a zit, but Thelma's voice urged caution and told me to breathe."

"She had that effect on all of us," I said, looking at my hands. "And now the bastards responsible are still out there."

Johns snapped out of his tranquil state. "All right, fine. I want to help you and the other guys out. Not much is happening in my world, so I wanted to know what you've found out so far."

"Johns, I know you are sincere about finding Thelma's killer, but you showing up here and asking to join us does raise some red flags. I have two guys who can give the FBI and CIA a run for their money. What do you have that we don't?"

"The law. Remember, you're still going for your PI license. Even if you do get it, that doesn't mean you can walk around the streets like you have a badge and a whole department backing you. What you and your small team doesn't understand is you can't run forever thinking nothing will happen to you." He tapped the table surface. "The only thing better than putting your head through the table is justice for Thelma."

It was my turn to take a moment to assess the situation. Sure, there would have been nothing better for me than to get up right then without replying and walk out of the place, but it wasn't the time to add more gasoline to the forest fire when they could be my ally. The guys were working hard decrypting the files while I sat with Johns, and chances are they would crack them sooner than the department's finest would. Johns could be the ace up my sleeve I would need later on when I did find Darren and Tony.

Also, I had to be careful what information I gave him. I wasn't ready to spill the tea on Kathleen and her current whereabouts. He might ask me in due time, but I had to play the whole thing like I was a blind man in the desert. There were too many problems that could arise if he found out I knew her location, and I didn't think Kathleen would be pleased if I was telling law enforcement her location. I had to keep his focus on finding Tony and Darren.

"Okay," I said, "we can help each other out, but Johns, I want to make it clear that this isn't a one-way street. If I find anything on Darren and Tony, I'll come to you, but you need to come to me if you find any gold nuggets."

He smirked and I wish he hadn't. "We got ourselves a deal."

Instead of shaking hands or making a blood oath, Johns gave me a slight nod as he got up from the table. He thanked Marie for the water and walked out of the place.

I lazily sat there for a while, replaying my conversation with Johns. Even the supposed tough cops have a heart after all, I concluded. I would occasionally look at my half-empty glass of water like it was going to magically fill up. Having Johns out there with emotional attachment sounded worse than before. The last thing I needed was a man of the badge running around with his own personal agenda. Hopefully, Johns would be smart enough to not get in the way, but I had to assume he was going to be around every corner I would be.

Needing to get back to Kathleen and the guys, I started to get up when a body sank into Johns' spot across from me. Thinking it was the cop, I sighed and started to lift my head. Instead of seeing Johns' pudgy face, I looked directly at a brown eye and a green eye. Darren Carver unblinkingly glared at me like we had a prearranged appointment. He gave me a blank stare as I went for my glass of water, ready to hurl it into his face.

"I'm not here to fight," he said, slowly lifting his hands. "Parlay."

"You're a pacifist now? Should have thought about that before becoming an accomplice to murder."

He shook his head. "I didn't want the old lady—"

"Thelma."

"Excuse me?"

"That 'old lady' had a name—Thelma."

He nodded. "Okay. I didn't want Thelma to die. The purpose of being there was only to scare her. We were meant to make it look like a robbery, but in the process talk to her about giving up the house and land, but Tony..." He sounded almost sick to say his name. "Tony took it too far. We were supposed to be gone by the time anyone showed."

"Who paid you to break into her place?"

"Tony told me about the job. Me and him have pulled off a number of jobs before, and he came up to me a few days before the break-in, asking if I could use extra cash. I thought, why not?"

"So, what happened?" I asked. I steadied my grip around the glass.

"We went in with a simple plan. We were only going to be in there a few minutes—me and Stephen tearing the place apart while Tony gave her a talking to. We came in through the back door, pulled her out of bed, and made her sit in the kitchen. While Stephen and I were turning over things in the living room, we started to hear shouting coming from the kitchen. This Thelma wasn't going to be bullied so easy. Tony screamed at her to sell the land, but she kept going on about how her husband built the place and that she would die there."

Darren stopped and looked at me as my face turned red.

Going to Mars seemed like an easier task than trying to cool down. My mind snapped back to the night I wanted scrubbed from my memory.

"So," I said, "tell me why I shouldn't scream at the owner to call the cops while I break every bone in your body?"

"Because I came here to warn you to get out of town now while things haven't boiled over yet. I've talked with Tony a few times since that night, and he told me powerful people are looking for you."

"Aren't you the thoughtful and concerned type."

"I know you're with Kathleen Newman." He didn't yell, but he had enough command in his voice that it felt like he had.

That gave me pause. I shouldn't have been surprised that he already knew given that I had tried my best to figure out who was tailing me, but that still didn't worry me into thinking about what he was planning to do next. My mind spun off in so many different directions that I had to remind myself to not let it show on my face.

He leaned back in his seat and studied the rest of the diner to make sure his voice hadn't reached all the walls, and then looked at me. "I saw you pick her up from the motel. I haven't told Tony yet that you found her."

Now Kathleen's safety was a foremost concern. I had known her hiding out at David and Goliath's was shaky to begin with, but all I could picture was more death when I returned to the apartment. Even though she was younger than Susan, Kathleen didn't show any signs of stopping or being easily bullied. She might not have been a professional when it came to going into hiding, but she had determination and didn't look like the type to be dragged away. She now understood there was more to what she carried on the thumb drive, so I knew here defenses would be heightened. I just had to figure out Darren's angle in all of this.

"Why haven't you?" I asked with steadiness.

"Like I said before, me and Tony had pulled off some jobs, but those were theft. Tony has been talking with a big-wig recently and it's gotten to his head. He believes he can kill his way to the top. He wasn't like this before. The man was all talk, but now he feels as if he's got the winning lottery ticket. He thinks taking care of you and Kathleen will usher him into high society. Also, I occasionally think about the sight of Thelma from that night. That was my first time seeing a dead body. I might be a crook, but that doesn't mean I'll kill anyone for possessions."

"So, is that why you put my head through a door and ran away—moral kindness?"

He waved that off. "I might not want people to die, but that doesn't exclude me from relaying messages, and if I have to do it physically, well." He shrugged. "I was going to tell you this before those kids ran up to the motel, shouting. All kids carry phones with them nowadays, so I didn't want to take that chance. I knew the hit wasn't going to give you brain damage. Just a physical message before a verbal one."

"What now?" I asked. "Are you having this talk with me, and then running out of town?"

He shook his head. "No. For me to leave now would be suspicious for everyone. That's why I'm here. If you and your new friend need to go far away for a period of time and let things die down, then I can casually move out with the wind."

"You must know that I can't leave. And Kathleen would probably agree with me. She's been moving from one motel to the next for the past week, but she hasn't left town. Now her feet are cemented to this town after the news about her sister."

"Yeah," he said with a reluctant sigh, "I was afraid you were going to say that."

"Did you kill Susan Newman?"

He snorted. "You haven't been listening to anything I've been telling you. I. Don't. Kill. People."

"But you know who did." I made that into a statement and not a question.

"My guess is Tony, but that was one job I was left out of. I can tell Tony is sensing I'm not on board with all his decisions. All I know is that Tony's been talking about other jobs he's been doing lately that were above my pay grade, as he put it. This is another reason why I'm waiting for my cue to leave, because I know I'll be dumped aside the second Tony had made it to the big leagues."

I went to say something, but ended up closing my mouth. If felt like I was being the unpaid therapist for a cop and a thief in the span of an hour. I still hadn't processed what Johns had told me and here was one of the thieves, practically sobbing to me because his man crush wasn't paying any attention to him. I shook it off, though, and continued talking with Darren, since our time together was limited.

I said, "Does this mean you are helping me now?"

"It means I'm giving you this warning because I was hoping you'd be smart enough to bail now and I could save my own ass. It seems to me that we are all in the long haul until one side gets their wish."

"If you want this to end, then tell me where I can find Tony."

He shrugged. "He moves around. We're not exactly best friends or roommates. Since the incident with Thelma, he hasn't stayed in one place. He's been setting up his own safe houses around town, and he makes sure not to stay in them for a certain amount of time. Every time I went to see him, he was in a different place."

"Why do I feel like you are playing both sides just to save your skin? Even if you make it out alive, you're still going to prison after

Tony is dealt with. It's obvious that the police know about you and will keep sending patrols out to your residence until you're caught."

Darren smiled. "They can keep going to that empty place all they like. I'm just protecting myself and making sure you and the police know what really happened that night. But I do plan on making it out by the end of everything."

I wanted to explain how full of shit he was, but even I couldn't predict his 3D chess game. I came out to get food and there I was having a chat with someone whose bones I wanted to break, and then toss into prison. Maybe he was playing mind games with me, but by the way his face sagged a little every time he brought up Tony, and the capabilities of Tony's strength, I thought there was some merit to his intel. I just had to add it to a list that I hadn't wanted or asked for.

Without saying anything more, like Detective Johns, Darren got up from the table nonchalantly and made his way out of the diner. He was the definition of inconspicuous, keeping his head down and avoiding eye contact with the other diners. Darren was out the door before anyone could put together who he was or accurately give his description later.

I finally got up from the table, leaving a twenty-dollar bill for Marie because I felt somebody should be paid for that quagmire hour.

16

Outside, the sky seemed to be loosening up some from the dark clouds, but I felt as if one was over my head and going to follow me around for some time. I started to make my way back to David and Goliath's place, knowing full well I didn't have any food for them, but not caring at the same time. My brain yelled at me to run back to the apartment, but my body walked like it needed me to consider different things. I didn't think they were in danger, but I wanted to tell them what had happened at the diner.

But what did happen? I kept taunting myself.

I had walked two out of the five blocks to the apartment when I spotted Chester leaning against the wall of a flower shop. He wore a ridiculous white cowboy hat. His head was tilted, but he slowly started to rise as I approached. He took a few steps forward when he saw me walking past him.

"Truman," he said, "Mr. Thornton would like to speak with you."

I half-turned. "Not in the mood, Chester."

"You don't have any option about it," he said, annoyed. "Mr. Thornton wants to speak with you now."

I looked around like I was trying to find Waldo. "Yeah, and where is Edmund? I'm not driving you to his office."

"You don't need to," he said as he snapped his fingers.

Half a moment later, an all-black stretch limousine pulled up next to us. I was surprised I hadn't noticed the monstrosity behind me as I had walked down the sidewalk. The thing took up almost half of the road, and even though it pulled up near the sidewalk, it still made it difficult for drivers to pass.

"Let's go," said Chester.

"Not today," I replied.

He grabbed my arm and started to pull me towards the limo. This was a great reminder that Chester was stronger and that I had a better chance of getting out of quicksand that out of his grip. I looked like a rambunctious child being dragged by an overbearing parent. Eventually, I just went with it, knowing I didn't have a chance. Chester opened the door and tossed me in like an empty backpack.

I picked my face off the leather seat after landing. I moved my head and looked around at the interior that cost more than any place I'd ever lived. There was a minibar to the left that held more bottles of wine and liquor than any average bar. The floor was carpeted and looked comfortable enough to sleep on. Along the rest of the limo were leather couches and seats, but they were mostly unoccupied.

Straight ahead, I found Edmund sitting with his legs crossed. He wore an expensive Italian suit that I guessed cost five times more than my car. He was drinking white wine and had the bottle open, appearing to be half gone. He took a swig, not caring if he got any on himself.

"Mr. Pierce," he said with a half-drunk smile. "I hope Mr. Watson wasn't too hard on you."

"Chester doesn't bother me," I said.

Chester put his arm around me like we were on a date, making sure I wouldn't fidget too much. The puppet didn't talk, but showed his physical strength. Edmund had trained him well.

"As much as you would like to show off this limo," I said, "I'm not interested in another talk about selling you Thelma's house and land."

Edmund took a swig. "Sorry, I'm being honored with a humanitarian award tonight. I forgot the name of it, they're all the same, but I'm trying to keep my suit as clean as possible—until afterwards, if you know what I mean." Edmund laughed. "Anyway, don't worry about that house or the land; in a matter of time, the courts will see it my way and will make sure that everyone will understand why the nephew of a well-respected woman of the community should lay claim to the property."

"You're a piece of shit," I hissed.

"Mad because you know there is no way for you to beat me, huh? A little man on the totem pole like yourself should know their place and stop trying to fight a person like me. Money is the ultimate power that breaks most people, and I intend to prove it once again with you."

I didn't respond.

He continued, "No, the reason we're having this conversation is to hire you."

It was my turn to laugh. "Ease up on the wine."

"You're not in my good graces right now, so finding this person will put you in, well, better faith with me."

"You've got plenty of resources, like this ape next to me." I said, nudging Chester.

He ignored me. "There's a woman who works at my company that has been missing for a while. I'd like your help finding her."

I stopped with the sarcastic routine and quickly put on my poker face. It was difficult to tell with Edmund's drunken state what he knew and what he didn't know. I eased myself a little, but didn't want Chester to think something was off because my muscles were too relaxed. I closed my mouth and opened my ears.

He continued, "Her name is Kathleen Newman and she's one of our accountants. She went missing some time ago. She's one of our star employees. Ms. Newman is the type of person who always shows up for work and excels at her job." Edmund burped and excused himself. "She's never had any trouble with the company before, and she isn't the type to vanish without telling anyone. Everyone at the company is very distressed by her sudden disappearance."

I said nothing.

"What do you make of this?" he asked.

I couldn't just sit there and keep quiet the entire time. The red flags would go up and the line of questions would turn towards grilling me and not her. Even if they were playing games with me, suspecting I knew where Kathleen was, I had to make sure to not give up any information and play the situation like I didn't know what they were talking about.

"When did you go to the police?" I asked.

"We haven't filed any report with the police yet."

I raised an eyebrow. "And why not? If she's your top employee and has been missing for more than forty-eight hours, someone would've gone to the police with this."

"My company and I want to make sure that we've done all we can before going to the authorities with this matter. As you can imagine, we don't want to stir any ruckus with local law enforcement only to find out Kathleen wasn't in any danger to begin with.

"When was the last time you saw her?"

"Me?" he asked with a puzzled look.

"Yes," I said, clearing my throat, "do you remember the last time you saw or spoke with her? I'm trying to get a sense of what she seemed like before she didn't show up to work the next day. Did you notice any problems with her?"

"No, she didn't appear to be distressed. And at the office, right up to when she disappeared, nobody ever said anything bad about her. I don't exactly recall the last time I talked to her since my business is normally outside of the office."

"You said she's an accountant? Did she deal with any sensitive materials?"

I didn't mean for the question to go in this direction, but while I sat there, I wanted to see what I could get. I was hoping Edmund might let something slip, but a man with his own company—and agenda—wasn't the easiest person to trip up.

"She didn't deal with top-secret information or anything," he said. "Kathleen helped with the budget and keeping the records straight. I have my own security detail that looks into classified information."

Chester made a grunting noise like he was proud to be working for the weasel.

"What do you think happened to her?" I asked. "You must have a theory about what happened."

Edmund lightly scratched his face. "Well, I believe it's something to do with her personal life. She wasn't the type to go around and talk about her problems with anyone. You kind of had to twist her arm to open up." He gave a short laugh. "She's one of many that's worked at my company who's done a good job of keeping their private life separate from their career."

"And that's all?" I was pushing my luck, but I didn't want to let up so easy.

"Yes, to my knowledge." He crossed his legs like he was turning it into a serious business meeting. "I know we've had our differences before, but I am willing to forget everything and pay you considerably to help find her."

"I would rather have the house and land," I replied.

"That is something I won't be able to stop. Like I said earlier, things are in motion and this is a system that is beyond your control. I hope you can understand this. What I can do is pay you for your troubles." He looked at me up and down. "It seems like a man in your position could benefit with some fortune."

All I could do was nod. My mind pictured me elbowing Chester in the face, and then giving Edmund many punches before Chester pulled me off. Edmund was testing me and the smirk on his face begged me to make a move. I breathed through my nose and kept the next part as cool as I could.

"I'll look into it," I said, "but I strongly recommend you go to the police with this information and file a report. This will help as I work with the police to combine resources to search for Ms. Newman." I even smiled for customer service.

Edmund returned the smile. "Yes, I'll make sure to contact the authorities when I can. Thank you, Mr. Pierce, for being able to keep a mature, level head about this." He motioned towards the door. "Now, if you don't mind, I have a ceremony to attend."

I looked at Chester. "That means you can let go of me and let me out, Gorilla."

Chester opened the door and tossed me out like I was a bag of trash. Luckily, I had my arms out and my face didn't land on the pavement. Just as I started to turn my head towards the limo, the machine was already around the corner and out of sight. I dusted myself off as people walked past me as if nothing had happened.

As I sprinted the remaining three blocks to David and Goliath's, my disdain for Edmund and the rest of his posse came to a boiling point. The arrogance coming from Edmund made me want to punch through a brick wall. It wasn't just his smugness, though; it was the fact that I had no clue how to bring him, or any of his people, down. It's the defeat you feel when the end hasn't happened, but all the walls have been erected and are preventing you from escaping the maze.

When I got back to the apartment, I found all three in the same spot as I had left them. The glowing computer screen stole their attention. They didn't hear me, but I was thankful it was me and not the people who wanted to do damage. After the talk with Edmund, I was more annoyed than ever that no one had locked the door. I shut the door harder than anticipated, causing them to rapidly turn in my direction. Kathleen gave a sigh of relief when she realized it was me.

"Didn't you grab any food?" asked Goliath.

I took one of the wooden chairs from the kitchen and sat in it after placing it next to a window. My back eased into the chair as I looked around the room, and then to the three of them. Each gave me a look like I had been kicked in the head multiple times. No one said anything, letting me collect my breath before speaking.

I laid out everything that had happened over the past hour. I went into how the cop, the crook, and the corporates were all converging on us because they each held a different piece of the puzzle. I explained how everyone, even Johns, made me feel they were watching us closer than anticipated. I didn't hold back on the details concerning Kathleen and how everyone would hunt her until there was a victor. When I got done with my talk, they gazed at me the same way as I was feeling.

"So," David said, "what do you think we should do next?"

That had been the same question racing through my head when I started talking to them about the past hour's activities. All I could see were dead ends, so I forced myself to slowly breathe in and out, cooling me down just enough so my mind wasn't hazy. I moved around the room, acting like the answers to my questions were under the chair or computer desk. As much as I enjoyed violent solutions running through my thoughts, I had to put all the juvenile notions to the side and find an answer that didn't involve my emotions. Goliath was ready to speak up when a light bulb went off in my head, making me raise my hand to stop him from speaking.

I said, "Goliath, how fast do you think you can put all the unencrypted documents we have so far on a USB drive?"

"Not long. Why?"

I peered at the three of them. "Edmund was dressed up, talking about going to some ceremony tonight."

"Yeah," interjected Kathleen, "he's supposed to be getting a humanitarian award."

"Right. So, the plan is for me and David to get into that event tonight. There should be a lot of people there with strong connections. Plus, enough reporters to spread some news. Normally these events have a projector of some sort, right?"

All three nodded in unison.

"So, we need to put the message into everyone's heads that Edmund Thornton and his company are dealing with unlawful behavior. The reason why Edmund thinks he's king of the world right now is that there isn't any damage to his armor. He's behind all of this, and that means we need to pressure him from other areas."

"But we don't have the rest of the files broken through yet," said Goliath. "We'll be painting bigger bulls-eye signs on our backs."

Kathleen said, "But if we just sit around and hope for things to happen, like I've been doing, then those same people will catch up to us, no matter what." She gave a look that mingled determination and hesitancy. "It's not exactly the best idea, but there aren't many we can go with right now."

"I'm not thrilled about this, either," said David. "It wouldn't be the best idea to just walk through the front door of the ceremony."

I shook my head. "It wouldn't. What do you think?"

David took out his phone and started to scroll through it like he was part of the machine. He typed faster than I could on a computer with three people helping. He did this for about a minute, then his eyes lit up.

"All right," he said, "the ceremony is being held in the downtown section at The Tanger. I know this hotel." He moved his head from side to side. "What we could do is put our names on the catering company's staff list and go in through the side entrance. We don't have to dress very fancy, but we need to make sure to grab a couple of the waiters' jackets there to help us blend in better."

"It's coming together." I turned to Goliath. "Can you get the information on the USB drive before we leave?"

Goliath said, "I just want to point out I'm not thrilled with this plan. With that said, it shouldn't take me too long."

"Good. Start putting together the files on the USB. When David and I head out for the event, keep digging into the encrypted files. Also, check to see if there's a guest list that David and I need to be on to get into the event. Some of these places won't let you in without certain clearances, and I don't want to show up there empty-handed."

Goliath nodded. "Will do. Still not crazy about this idea."

I ignored him as Kathleen walked up to me with a determined face. I had just met her, but I assumed this was the most focused she had ever been.

"And what do you want me to do?" she asked.

"For now, stay here with Goliath and help with the files. I would say come along with me and David to the event, but your face is on more than just milk cartons. When we get back, we'll see what to do next."

She nodded and sat down next to Goliath, asking him how she could help.

"What should we wear for the ceremony?" asked David as he approached me.

"Let's just get a couple of black ties, white shirts and dark slacks. We don't have to transform completely, just enough to blend in."

"All right. I have extra clothes if you want to borrow them."

I thanked him.

David looked at the others, then back at me. "I'm hopeful that things will work out."

"So am I."

How many times was I going to try to convince myself?

17

A few hours later, David and I were at the event in our matching attire. We made sure to park a few blocks away from the event. Goliath had texted me en route to assure us that there wasn't any list for the catering crew, but there was a good amount of security.

When we got to The Tanger, we went straight to the alley and found four black and white vans with "Howard's Catering" marked on the sides. The rich pockets attending the event were around the corner, getting their pictures taken and pretending they were so happy to be helping the community and honoring someone like Edmund Thornton. You could hear the crowds going wild for every limousine dropping off the next pile of people they desperately wanted to become.

There were a few people bringing in boxes of food, so me and David wasted no time jumping in. We hurried over to the first van where a Hispanic man was just unloading a tray of food. We were fortunate to see that his attire was pretty much identical to our—minus the blazer he wore. He looked at us and smiled, handing each of us a tray. Without a word, I took a tray, and then David followed suit. There was a group of people by the entrance, so I lowered my head like a good servant and was able to pass without any trouble.

Inside, we went through the industrial kitchen, putting our

trays down with ease on a silver-surfaced kitchen island. Luckily, there were several red vests hung up near the entrance door, so me and David each took one, nonchalantly. We put them on, keeping our stature of well-disciplined servants. I then ushered us over to an area of the room where we were just far enough from everyone to have a quick conversation. Most of the staff was moving in and out of the kitchen, while the six cooks had their heads focused on the meal preparation, oblivious to the surrounding world.

"All right," I said, "do you have the USB drive on you?"

Without looking at anyone in the room, David slowly took out the drive and held it a few inches from his pocket, our Holy Grail. He gave me a nod to make sure I understood.

"Good," I said. "Remember: wait for Edmund to reach the podium. Once you start playing the file, get out as fast as you can. Don't wait for me. Make sure you can quickly make it out before security can get their hands on you. We'll meet back at your place."

David didn't say anything, but I could tell the pressure was putting a squeeze on him. Beads of sweat were moving down the sides of his face. His cheeks turned red and there was a nervous twitch of his left eye. He kept his breathing relatively calm, but I was afraid he would start hyperventilating soon.

"Just remember that you aren't the main attraction," I said. "You won't have to make the big presentation when the USB starts doing its work."

He half-smiled and gave a nod.

"You go out first, and then I'll make my way out in a minute." I lightly shook my head. "Also, if you feel there's anyone tailing you or the heat is around the corner, drop what you're doing and get out. But don't turn every little thing you see into something suspicious. Okay?"

He gave another nod.

David cracked open the door to the main area and looked through like he was a mouse. He did this for a few seconds before opening the door a couple of feet and squeezing through.

When I was by myself, I scanned a quick panoramic view of the room. Thankfully, no one was staring at me or walking up to me to ask questions. The wait staff and the cooks were still scrambling around like this was the last event they would ever cover. They worked in unison, cooking the food and making sure there were enough trays, plates, and utensils for the people overpaying to be there. You could tell many of them had been doing this line of work for years by how they were able to maneuver through the frenzy without constantly bumping into one another. I even started to move around like them without being a distraction.

After a few minutes, the waiters and waitresses started making a line while the chefs prepared hors d'oeuvres on silver trays. The chefs moved fast, making the line shrink rapidly. I jumped into the back. When it was my turn, a chef with blue eyes and a no-nonsense attitude practically hurled the tray at me. I didn't waste any time gazing at the man while picking it up. I made sure to hold the tray up with one hand, mimicking the person in front of me. I kept my pacing quick but professional.

I followed the line into the lobby, outside of the banquet hall. The ceremony was scheduled to start soon, but there was already a large crowd gathered. There were a few flowers and decorations displayed to show there was some event happening, but nothing over-the-top. The wait staff spread out on cue and started to serve each guest. The area was smaller than I anticipated, giving the crowd a tighter space to work with. It was good to blend in, and I wasn't giving anyone a chance to point me out.

I decided to hang back close to the wall, staying as near to as many guests as possible. There were several security personnel within the crowd, making me keep my back to them as much as I could. I didn't fear that my face was on their phones for a person to apprehend when found, but I certainly didn't want to wave my hand in the air and announce myself. I didn't hesitate to oblige every guest that either stuck their hand out to the tray or waved me down. There were plenty of people who were rude to me, but I wasn't going to let my pride get the best of me, especially since I knew why I was there and it wasn't an audition to work for the catering company.

I wasn't familiar with the layout of the building, but as I gazed around the room, I saw a door the same color as the beige walls next to the all-white double doors for the banquet hall. My assumption was that this might be the stairs that led up to the projection room or something similar. My only hope was that David had made it to the room before the room swelled with guests. It wouldn't be smart for me to hang around that door to try to get on the other side.

"God, can you believe this bullshit gig?" said a voice behind me.

I turned and a guy who looked to be in his early twenties with dark hair and oily skin was looking at me. He was dressed similar to me and held a tray filled with hors d'oeuvres that appeared to have a mix of broken chicken with a cut tomato resting on top. I had already made up my mind not to guess the type of food we were serving. I looked at my new coworker as he kept talking.

"This might be my second catering gig, but I just want to throw this tray against the wall and tell all these rich pricks to go fuck themselves." He said the last part in a whisper.

I said, "If so, make sure to throw the tray as far from me as possible. I need this job."

"And that's the problem. We are the ones being screwed by the system and these people know all about it."

He kept talking, but my mind was on the projection room and

banquet hall. I needed to blend in as much as I could, so triggering my opinionated coworker and having him make a scene wasn't an option. Thankfully, there weren't any guests looking with suspicion in our direction. After about a minute of him talking while I acted like I was listening, he started to ease away from his rant.

"Okay," he said, "gotta get back to serving the snobs." He leaned into my ear. "By the way, I have some coke in my breast pocket. Let's do a line later."

Before I could politely decline his request, he scurried away.

For the remaining time before the event started, I kept my head down and hoped David was able to make it to the projection area without any trouble. I kept picturing security rushing to the opposite part of the building and dragging David away in handcuffs.

Finally, someone from the banquet hall announced the ceremony was about to start, and the crowd moved casually through the double doors. The looks on their faces either said they were happy to be there or they felt it was part of their parole. People passed me, putting whatever trash they held onto the tray. This was a good reminder to maintain my neutral face as I quietly thanked them when they didn't bother to acknowledge me.

Not knowing what to do next, I stayed where I was just as the last person went into the banquet hall. Still holding the tray, I was about to ask someone the next step when all the wait staff started to hustle back into the kitchen. This time, I made sure not to be the last one into the room, so I eased my way into the small crowd.

In the kitchen, people with trays started to stack them near the sink after emptying whatever was left into the garbage. I continued to mimic everything they did and didn't take any time getting it done. After stacking my tray, I saw a few pitchers of iced water on the island table. I thought this would be a great way to get into the banquet hall, but several waiters and waitresses started to hurry towards them. I moved fast, lightly pushing a number of waiters out of the way. I grabbed the last pitcher, beating out a portly man who huffed in despair.

A man with a salt-and-pepper beard and aviators put his up arms to get everybody's attention. "Everyone, the main course is running a few minutes behind schedule. The chefs are getting everything together, but I want the water servers to go out there and reassure patrons that their meals will be done shortly."

Once again, I moved with everyone else like an ant in a line. The bearded man took a look at me and gave me a suspicious look. He started to reach out and grab my shoulder, but one of the chefs raced up to him and huffed that they'd run out of carrots. The bearded man shot a worried look to the chef and planted the same hand he had almost grabbed me with on the chef's shoulder. I didn't stick around to hear their problems.

I was the last to go through the double doors, but when I did, I was impressed by how the banquet hall looked completely different from the rest of the building. There were several round tables and mahogany chairs scattered throughout the room with white, silk table cloths that appeared to be specially made for the event. The walls looked freshly painted in satin white and with large, framed pictures of either Edmund or his charitable work hung throughout the room. There were a couple of chandeliers hanging from the ceiling that appeared to have been imported. The front of the room had a podium with an assortment of flowers lined up against the wall. When I entered, there was a woman with thick glasses who appeared to be in her sixties welcoming everyone to the event.

What I was thankful to see was behind the woman, right above the flowers: an assortment of images being projected onto a theater-size screen. First, I saw a picture of Edmund in his twenties in the shot, but then it changed to another shot after ten seconds. My eyes followed the light from the screen to the upper level where I found a small window. There was a projector with a laptop hooked up to it, but I couldn't make out anything or anyone else. I only hoped David was already there, but I had to remind myself to not stare and to be a good servant for the guests.

Upfront, slightly towards the right from the projection screen, was the man of the hour. Edmund sat at a table with many faces I had seen on TV or on news sites. These were the people who ran the town and were the gatekeepers to the town's operation. From where I stood, I could see a couple of council members and the chief of police. Other people I didn't recognize, but where they sat meant they had deep enough pockets to influence the top citizens. And even without the cowboy hat, you could spot Chester from a mile away sitting next to Edmund. Lucky for me, most of his back was turned and he was busy sucking up to the other guests.

I started with the tables in the back, filling up their water glasses as quick and precise I could without lingering. I didn't want to rush anything, but I didn't want anyone to start asking me questions and call in security before I had the chance to do what needed to be done.

Security was dressed in suits like Secret Service, doing their best to hide their earpieces so they'd be inconspicuous. You would've thought they were protecting the president with their discrepancy. I knew I wasn't on their radar, because a few of them looked at me and made no move to escort me out. I wasn't going to arouse any suspicions until the time came.

"Excuse me," said a man tugging at my arm. He looked to be around fifty and had a pudgy face.

"How can I help you, sir?" I asked.

He motioned to his empty glass.

Instead of telling him to fill the glass himself, I smiled and apologized.

Studying the room had made me forget I was holding the water pitcher. I eased the pitcher so that I wasn't blocking the view or making any sound louder than water going into the glass. I did my best being a shadow as I moved around the table and filled up each glass the fastest I could without spilling any onto the table. I was just thankful that my hands were steady and didn't get me into unnecessary trouble.

Moving to another table, I repeated the same process. I had to keep my senses around me sharp, but also keep moving and not just stand around. I thought about the next couple of steps I had to make when it was my turn. I knew what I was going to say, but I had to make sure I had plenty of time to get it done without being tackled.

David and I had never discussed any signal for when he got to where he needed to be. I knew that when he turned on the file, then it was go time, but for all I knew, he had probably been taken into another room by Edmund's security and was getting the shit knocked out of him. While filling up another glass, I decided that if that was the case, then I would turn and walk out quietly after Edmund's speech.

It finally came closer to curtain time when the woman at the podium excused herself for a brief moment to listen to another suit whisper in her ear.

"Ladies and gentlemen," she said, talking into the microphone again, "Our evening's dinner is running a little late, so we're going to switch our order of ceremonies." She motioned towards Edmund. "Let me introduce the man of the evening, Mr. Edmund Thornton."

The crowd applauded a frenzy as Edmund got up from his seat and made his way to the podium. He took his time, nodding a few times to the crowd like he was impressed by their response. Edmund looked my way a few times, but I made sure to act like I was still pouring water so his eyes swept past me. When he stood at the podium, he raised his arms a little to bask in the glow. I wanted to take the remaining water I had and throw it on him.

"Thank you, ladies and gentlemen," he said as he lowered his arms.

Edmund started on his speech, but I turned towards the projector. Behind the laptop, I saw something move in the background. I couldn't make out who it was, but I was optimistic at that moment and pictured David getting ready. The pictures behind Edmund as he spoke were more of the humanitarian work he claimed to be a part of.

I wasn't as worried about Edmund looking in my direction at that moment compared to the security that kept watch. They moved a little more now like they were planning to find a sniper under one of the tables. Whenever they moved, I made sure to casually walk over to another table and pretend they desperately needed water.

Over a minute into Edmund's speech I started to worry about David and whether this was going to happen. Time seemed to be slowing down, and it wasn't good that I was running out of water in my pitcher. Most of the wait staff had already retreated back to the kitchen. It was starting to feel like I was alone on a deserted island. Sweat ran down my face and my muscles tensed like they were working out. I felt the eyes of security floating towards me.

Edmund could speak for an hour, but I knew my time had run out, so I turned and started for the exit. I kept my head low and quietly excused myself for either bumping into someone or being in their view of Edmund. My hand reached for the door handle when someone in the audience spoke up.

"What is that?" they yelled.

I turned and found one of the pages David had put onto the USB lighting up the projection screen. It was a page that connected Edmund to bribing a local cop to look the other way so unknown individuals could trespass on a person's private residence. The crowd pointed and talked over Edmund. Even Edmund was so shocked he took a few steps back to get a better look at what was on the wall. I knew I didn't have much time until the power on the projector was gone, so I set the pitcher down and made my way to the center of the room.

"That," I yelled, "ladies and gentlemen, is proof of fraud from the same person you decided to honor with a humanitarian award tonight." I projected my voice over the other people talking so they would all turn in my direction.

Security turned my way, leaving me only a short time to skip introductions and get right to the point.

"Edmund Thornton has deceived all of you." I pointed to the screen. "Here is just a taste of the proof I have that shows Thornton's direct connection to illegally obtaining land throughout town by means of fraud and embezzlement."

Some of the crowd got to their feet to either get a better look at me or tell me to shut up. The reporters and other members of the crowd wasted no time in taking out their phones and pointing their cameras in my direction.

Edmund just stood in place, but Chester was on his feet and moving with the rest of security like snakes through the crowd. They weren't running, but the look in their eyes said they were going to do more than just escort me out.

I continued, "Soon, I will provide evidence that Mr. Thornton and people in his company are connected to murder and other high-level crimes."

Chester and the rest of security had me practically surrounded not far from where I stood. As they closed in, I took out the picture of Thelma holding her baby nephew and held it up to Edmund.

"This is Thelma Reilly and she was gunned down recently by people connected with Edmund Thornton." I lifted the photo as high as I could. "Look, Edmund, at the person who would've given you the world, and all you gave her was death."

I put the picture back into my pocket just as the first guard reached out to grab me. I ducked and spun to the exit with no one blocking the door. Chester yelled for someone to grab me, but I was already halfway to the exit. I felt two of the guards close to me, breathing down my neck. I opened one of the double doors, and then closed it before anyone could catch me.

In the lobby, there were a few guests looking at me like they wanted an explanation for all the commotion. I looked towards the kitchen for a possible escape, but the staff finally had the entrees ready for the guests, blocking any straight getaway. The doors started to swing open behind me, so on impulse, I ran down the hallway with no one in the way.

Yells either screaming for me to stop or screaming for others to catch me sounded like they were inches behind me, making me run faster. I wasn't sure what was down this hallway until I found a door marked "STAIRS." I pushed through and found that they not only went to the upper levels, but also around the stairs was an exit door. I sprinted around the stairs and pushed on the door.

My eyes adjusted to the newly-formed dark sky, but when I did, the back alley materialized. I found David across the way, but as I took a couple of steps out to join him, his face changed from relief to shock. Before I got a chance to turn, something hit the back of my head, slamming my eyes shut.

And my world turned black.

18

Throbbing pain in the back of my head was the first thing I noticed before any of my other senses kicked in. It felt like a bowling ball was glued to the back of my head. My eyes opened slowly and all I could see, at first, was blurry darkness. Soft sounds crept into my ears after I thought I'd become deaf. I went to touch the back of my head, but quickly realized my hands were bound behind my back. The material binding my wrists felt like duct tape. All I could make out through the blurry darkness was my outline tied to a chair. My strength was diminished, so there wasn't any point in attempting to rip out of my constraints.

Across the dark room, a voice I recognized talked to someone.

"Yes, sir," Chester said, "Pierce is with me now." A few seconds of silence passed. "I guarantee none of the reporters or anyone else saw me drag him away. I had the car ready and was able to get him out before people knew what had happened. Yes, I'll make sure to find out what I can by any means. I'm not alone."

I saw the glow of the cell disappear. Chester spoke up when he heard me squirm in the chair.

"Finally awake, Pierce?" he asked.

Chester flipped on a switch, turning on a bulb directly above my head. It was weak, but it still made my eyes close to adjust to the difference in light levels. When my eyes decided the light was fine,

I looked around me. I sat in a relatively new residential basement that seemed to be around 300 square feet. The walls were painted light blue and the beige carpet didn't have any stains, nor had it faded. The only furniture I could make out were a few metal chairs and a raggedy square table with four metal legs.

When my eyes fully adjusted, Darren was standing against the wall with his arms crossed. His mismatched eyes gave me the same look one does with a disobedient child. He didn't say anything, but spoke a novel's depth to me through his facial expression. I could tell he wanted to scream at me for not getting out of town and ignoring all his other advice.

"You can scream all you want," said Chester, "but the owners were bought out by Mr. Thornton a long time ago, as well as the surrounding neighbors."

I looked straight ahead and found Chester sitting in a similar chair. He wasn't wearing his cowboy hat, but still had his cell in his hand. Instead of giving me his usual scowl, he looked upon me like this was his checkmate.

"Decided you didn't want to get blood on your hat?" I asked.

He ignored me. "It seems like you have been keeping a number of things from us. Mr. Thornton was gracious enough to give you a chance to become a part of our team. Now those terms are void."

"Spare me the talk and just kill me before I die of boredom."

He smirked. "As much as I would like to spend the rest of the night slowly hacking away at your body, I'm here on something bigger than yourself." He leaned towards me. "Where did you get those documents?"

Instead of answering, my leg started to vibrate. I realized my phone was still in my pocket. He hadn't taken my phone away? They hadn't noticed? I imagined it was one of the guys calling me after David witnessed my lights getting knocked out. They could track me, I thought, but what did the duo actually think they could do once they found me? Also, I didn't think this conversation would go all night. Neither Chester nor Darren made any indication of my cell vibrating in my pocket. I kept my face trained on Chester.

He said, "We can skip past my next couple of questions and you can tell me where Kathleen Newman is currently located."

"And why would I do that?"

"So, you're not denying it?"

"Of course not. Those documents didn't just drop on my head. We both know who gave them to me. And I won't waste your time saying I'm not telling you where she is."

He eased back in his chair, looking slightly away from me. "I'm actually impressed because we had been looking for her for quite some time now, using all our resources, but never got any good leads. And here's this lowlife who found her in no time."

"Well, she had good reason to stay away from you, and it didn't take long for me to convince her I was on her side."

I wanted to say more, but a noise came from my left. I hadn't noticed it before, thinking Chester, Darren, and myself were the only ones in the room, but it was apparent we had another guest. Behind a closed door, I heard a toilet flush.

"Does Edmund himself need to come and make his point?" I asked.

Chester smirked. "Not exactly. Mr. Thornton won't be involved in any discussions from here on out. He's excused himself from all activities, and now I will be taking over the next course of action."

While the person in the bathroom took their sweet time, Chester stood up and started to move around leisurely. He looked down at me like he wanted to squash me with his boot.

"You probably know that I spent some time in the Marines, correct?"

"I did my research on you."

"Then you must know that during my time I gained knowledge on interrogating suspected terrorists. It was only a few months, but people really catch on quick when they gain certain rights and permissions to do what is good for civilization."

Chester didn't speak for a few moments as he walked around until he stood right behind me. His height cast a shadow over me. I tried to turn my head, but all I could get was his outline. He started to poke my shoulders and arms, but then he grabbed onto my pinky finger.

He said, "When interrogating someone, you don't want to go for the face or anything that might make the suspect blackout. What you want is to start small, like the pinky finger, so you can show the suspect they have a long road ahead." He squeezed my finger. "There are three bones in your pinky finger. This is the best place to start because it gives the suspect three examples right away about how far someone like me would take it. Then—"

"And then you work around my entire body, breaking every bone until I spill whatever I know to you." I sighed. "You can break my bones, but nothing is going to change and you'll just end up wasting your time. This is more about the sick and twisted game you want to enact on me."

Chester laughed as he let go of my finger. "And then there are prisoners like you. Yes, I could eventually break you if given the time, but time is one thing I don't have. There is more than just physical force we could use to break people like you." He tapped me on the head. "It's here that can be broken when given enough pressure. Not physical, but enough emotions for your mind to crack sufficiently."

Just as Chester said the last part, the bathroom door opened. At first, all I could see was the outline of a figure. The person stood in the doorway for a few seconds, clearly eyeing the situation in progress. I started to open my mouth, but the stranger moved a few feet into the light. He stood with his shoulders back and head straight. His face was clean-shaven but carried an anger that could scare the devil. I formed a mental mask around the stranger's face, and then I knew exactly who the mystery guest was.

Tony.

My body started to react, but Chester put his hands on my shoulders and held me down tighter than a seatbelt as Tony walked across the opposite side of the room. He stood next to Darren as both looked upon me like they were a jury made of killers. Tony and I both looked at each other, neither of us blinking. His eyes had the same unshaken and deadpan gaze I encountered the night he had murdered Thelma. He was the type of person you could feel the evil rising off of from several blocks away. He leaned against the wall with his arms crossed.

"I didn't realize it was the same Truman Pierce I've read about," he said.

"I'm going to kill you," I growled.

His sights stayed on me. "You're lucky I'm not going to kill you tonight. If I had known last time, I would've done it. You look—and still do—like a faceless person you pass on the street."

Chester said, "Your mind is already starting to break, Truman. I didn't think you would have this reaction so soon, given your tough attitude. Do you still want to die or do you have a reason to keep going?"

"What I want is for you to untie me and give me a few minutes with this murderer." I twisted my wrists like my constraints would magically fall off.

Tony smiled, showing off a pair of white dental implants. He took a few steps forward, reached behind his waistband, and pulled out the Colt Python he had used to kill Thelma. He raised the gun to his chest, the barrel pointed towards the bathroom. His eyes traced the instrument like it was a beacon of hope.

"Normally, I like to get rid of all weapons I use on a job," said Tony, "but this one I just can't seem to let go. It's a sin to just toss this in the river or throw it in the garbage. I took this gun off a bookie after slitting his throat. People react different to this than they do when I use a nine-millimeter Glock or Beretta. Someone who sees this knows there isn't any turning back."

He knelt down so we were face-to-face. Tony raised the cannon and placed the barrel firmly under my chin, lifting my head some. Chester made sure to squeeze my shoulders as a reminder I wasn't going anywhere. A foot away from his face, Tony's eyes seemed to get darker. I mimicked his facial expression and betrayed no fear.

He continued, "This is the perfect place for a gun of this caliber to get the job done. You of all people know this. Some of my most beautiful work happened that night with the old bitch. It didn't matter if she was a three-hundred-pound Olympian, this would have still given us the same result. I keep all six chambers loaded at all times, but one is more than enough to get the job done."

"Here's what's going to happen, Pierce," said Chester, still holding me down. "You've got twenty-four hours to find Kathleen and hand her over to us with everything she's stolen. You might not know where she is now, but you can find her better than anyone else."

He continued to talk, but I just sat there and my mind went through how I could trap all three of them without any further escalation. Before, I had felt comfortable knowing I was a few steps ahead of them, but now they were sprinting and had almost caught up to me. The element of surprise was mostly gone, but I had to keep my mind on the half-glass-full approach as they didn't know where Kathleen was at the moment or realize that their world was close to crumbling.

As for Tony, this was the second time he had the upper hand on me. I didn't know what was running through his head—besides death—but I had to stop treating him like he wasn't a planner. There was no doubt he did more than just pull the trigger and take the money afterwards. He'd made it this far because he understood how the system operated, and he knew exactly where he could and couldn't take his steps. I had seen his face now, but that didn't mean anything when he knew how to hide in the shadows and wait like a tiger before striking.

"Do you understand me, Pierce?" asked Chester.

I nodded like I was paying attention. "Yeah, understood."

Tony moved to align our eye contact with each other. "If you don't do what he says, Truman, then you will see me one more time. And if that happens, you won't be walking away."

He finally backed away from me. I was going to say something about his bad breath, but he seemed like the type looking for any excuse to use the Colt—whether following directions or not. He only took a few steps back, but I kept my eyes on him.

Darren made no noise or movements throughout the whole ordeal to the point I had forgotten he was in the room. He was still in his statue pose, making sure not to add anything to what was already a difficult night. He had more to say than Chester and Tony combined, but he kept his Zen-like silence going. He didn't snap out of his tranquil state until Chester talked to him.

"Untie him," commanded Chester.

"Before he does," said Tony. He balled his hand into a fist and threw it across my face. "Just a reminder for you."

Chester and Tony walked out, leaving me with Darren. The side of my head where Tony had hit me was pounding. My vision was doubled, but I closed my eyes before I became dizzy enough to vomit.

All I wanted was to break free and make a run for Tony, but there was no doubt they were prepared for that approach. I saw the two standing on the other side of the door, Tony holding the Colt after I had opened the door and giving me a smile before pulling the trigger. I had to assume they had every angle planned out.

I was still running the different scenarios of how to get the upper hand when I felt Darren tearing my restraints off my wrists. I didn't even see or hear him walk over. He was taking his time untying me, close enough to my ear to whisper.

"You really know how to take advice, don't you?" he said.

"I wasn't going to run that fast," I said, mirroring his whisper.

"You have Kathleen. Get out of town with her, fly to Antarctica and stay there until the polar icecaps melt."

"I'm close to breaking Edmund Thornton and his whole operation. I should be telling you to get out of town."

He grabbed my wrist and twisted, making me bite my lip. "You still don't understand who these people are," he said. "They are the ones who create the game and decide who plays and who doesn't. Your only option is to run."

"And let the murderers walk free?"

He let go of my wrist. "As opposed to you ending up like Thelma? Simple answer."

I sighed as Darren worked to tear off the remaining duct tape. We had different views of the problem, but neither of us could convince the other why their plan was better. He could try to convince me all night, but he wasn't going to change my mind when I knew David and Goliath were working away at the files until I could show them to the world, but time wasn't cooperating with me.

"Am I going to just walk out of here?" I asked Darren as he moved to my side.

"Not exactly."

He pulled out an all-black stocking mask from his pocket. Darren threw it over my face without saying anything more.

19

My body sat up straight in the backseat of a moving car. No one said anything, and the car's engine was all the noise we could hear. It seemed as if we were driving all over the state with no intention of slowing down. I figured the darkness I was experiencing with the mask was no different than the same night the others in the car were experiencing.

They kept me held against the door, and a few times I tried to feel for the handle but kept stopping myself because I didn't think I would get too far if I actually made a break. Also, someone sat next to me, occasionally bumping into me whenever we made a turn. This would cause the person to shove my head against the window, whether on purpose or not, but I figured this was done more for theatrics than just accidental bump-ins. This type of force could only come from Chester.

After what felt like hours in the car, the machine started to slow down as someone reached across me and opened the door. I was ready to step out when the car slowed, but instead I was pushed out of the moving car. I rolled a couple of times on the pavement until I hit some empty trashcans. I lay there for a few seconds as I heard the car speed off.

I took the mask off and tossed it beside me. I knew right away that I was still a few miles away from my place. I was closer to the outskirts, sitting in front of someone's townhouse as I got up and dusted myself off. I took this as a win because they hadn't dropped me off at David and Goliath's, and then, given them the same treatment as me, and then dragged Kathleen away.

I started for my place, staying to the sidewalk and hurrying as fast as I could even though my leg was bothering me after the fall. I took out my phone, thinking the machine was broken in a dozen pieces. Besides a few scratches, the phone was working well. I saw there were several missed calls from David, Goliath, and Detective Johns. I decided to call David first as he was the one had seen me being abducted and would be the one who hacked into the NSA to try and find me. He picked up on the first ring.

"Truman!" he yelled into the phone.

I put the phone an inch from my face, then put it back. "Yeah, I was just released by Chester and his buddies, Tony and Darren."

"You...well." He coughed as he formulated his next question. "Where are you?"

"They dropped me off a few miles away from my place. I'm heading there now."

"Good, because Kathleen is there right now."

I stopped walking. "What do you mean she is there? Why isn't she with you guys?"

"She freaked out after I got back and told her and Goliath about what happened to you. She started getting paranoid, saying she couldn't stay here. I was able to reason with her in a short time and told her to go to your place. I even gave her a key to the house. I figured that would be the last place anyone would look for her. The motels must be crawling with Edmund's people."

I wanted to be mad at him, but he did have a point. If there was any place for her to go on short notice and without the whole nation keeping watch, it would be the basement of a house where a gruesome murder had recently taken place. They probably even drove by the place, not realizing she was right under their noses.

I nodded like he could see me. "All right, that was a good call. I'm guessing she took all her stuff with her, including the encrypted files?"

"She didn't. Thankfully, she trusted me and Goliath enough to give us the electronic files to decipher. She took the printed materials, but I figured what we needed was on the USB drive. She made sure to split it up so if she did get caught, she would only have the materials that have already been made available. Goliath is here, still trying to crack the files. It looks like he hasn't moved since he sat down."

I heard Goliath's voice from a distance say he hadn't.

"And where are you guys with those files?" I asked. "The clock is starting to speed up."

"It's going well. Goliath said he thinks he's close to finding a hidden key that will unlock all the files at once. We're hoping we can crack the code within twenty-four hours."

I gave a sigh of relief. "Just what I wanted to hear. Lock the doors and make sure no one gets in. If you get into any trouble, call either Longhorn or Johns."

David moved closer to the microphone. "Before you go, you need to hear this. The stunt tonight has been going all over the web and news sites. I've been following how people are starting to question Edmund. Now, a few of these sites are already calling you another crazed protestor, but a number of journalists are doing their jobs for a change and have started digging into the validity of our information. We sent in the same documents you showed tonight to several outlets and they are checking authenticity. Several of them are already requesting more proof about Edmund and his company."

I shook my head in agreement. "Good. Do whatever you and Goliath can about the remaining files. I'll be in touch."

David told me he would, and then I hung up.

Next up, I called Detective Johns. Even though I knew the call would be short, it was one I hadn't wanted to make because I knew he would make my head hurt more than it already did. Just like David, he answered on the first ring. I made sure to keep the speaker a few inches away from my ear.

"What the hell have you done?" screamed Johns.

I put the phone back to my ear. Before he could keep screaming, I went straight into my abduction and everything the cameras didn't pick up after the banquet hall. I made sure to put a lot of emphasis on Tony and how he had confessed to every crime committed since we had gotten involved. During my description of the past few hours, I could hear Johns' breathing get quieter and quieter until I believed there was no one on the other side of the line.

"All right," he said, taking in a breath, "I've given Longhorn a few breadcrumbs about the situation. We're working on picking up Tony."

"How much trouble am I in?" I asked.

"Surprisingly, not much. There was a patrol car that went by your house, but it didn't see anyone there. It would've been a big deal if those documents you showed were nothing, but a lot of people are in a frenzy because they seem to be legit. The police station is already in a panic, thinking there's going to be another police-station purge like last year. They'll want to talk with you soon, but the potential corruption of law enforcement and other government officials has taken precedent."

I took in a breath. "That buys me some time. The guys are working on the files. Try to stall things as much as you can. I just talked to David and he said it won't take much longer. Let

Longhorn know I'm not going anywhere and will be compliant when everything comes to light."

"Yeah, I'll keep the dogs away for now," he said with annoyance.

We both hung up and I started to quicken my pace back to the house.

My body might've been walking in the direction of the house, but my mind was on another planet. I hadn't expected to be faced with Tony during the second part of my night. There was always the risk of being caught, but I took that as spending the night in a jail cell. My skin turned to fire thinking of Tony with the loaded gun and my own helplessness. It wasn't enough that Chester had caught me, but it added a new level that Tony was on standby, ready for another encounter. I would've kept walking all night, but as soon as my mind switched back to Kathleen, my legs quickened to the house. The possibility of Tony stepping back into the crime scene reawakened my muscles like a defibrillator.

When I reached the house, I saw from a short distance a faint light coming from one of the basement windows. Thankfully, David had told me who my house guest was so I didn't get another surprise. I walked along the outside of the house, casually looking behind me just in case someone waited to tackle me. The moon cast a spotlight effect on the walkout basement door, like I had finally made it to the finish line. I stumbled a little as I reached for the knob, but I slowly pushed on the door so that Kathleen wouldn't get spooked.

The light from the kitchen was on, but there was no sign of Kathleen. You could tell with the room's calmness that there had been a presence inside not more than a few seconds before I had arrived. The kitchen chair moved just enough to indicate someone had just vacated it and one of the cupboard doors was half open.

"Kathleen, it's Truman," I said in a soft but firm voice.

Kathleen walked around the corner of the staircase. She wore a pair of white sneakers that matched her jeans and T-shirt. She carried only a few personal items with her, but eased them down to the ground. Kathleen looked to have aged ten years since I last saw her a few hours ago. Her blue eyes seemed to have faded away, leaving a more gray-like color. Her worried face didn't change when she saw me standing alone.

"I thought you were dead," she said. She trembled getting the words out.

I kept my place at the door, not wanting to make any sudden movements to jar her further. This wasn't the same person I had met at the motel. Her sister's death and the files' jeopardy had exploded in her psyche. She was the mouse hiding in a house full of cats. I had to reassure her.

"You and me both," I said. "David told me you were here. No one else is going to be here tonight but me and you. If you want, I can find you a place tonight where you can be alone and safe."

She shook her head. "That won't be necessary."

"Or I can leave you here. I have no reason to believe anyone will come by here tonight."

"No!" she yelled as she ran up to me. "Please don't go anywhere. I've been on edge since leaving the techs' apartment. I don't want to be alone now."

I lightly rested my hands on her shoulders. "I'm not going anywhere. How about we sit on the couch before you collapse?" I said the last part with a smile.

She gave me a faint smile. "My body feels like it's going to collapse."

Kathleen wasn't lying when she said that. She fell onto the couch as I sank down like a senior citizen. She breathed in and out, meditation-class style, as my muscles stopped burning. We didn't say anything to each other for the first minute. The raggedy couch was as good as a beach in Bermuda for both of us. I used the opportunity to change subjects and get away from the dark shadows in Kathleen's head.

"Did you bring your closetful of clothes with you?"

She tried to laugh, but it came out as a hiccup. "There are still a few bags in your car, but I have my essentials by the staircase." She took in a breath. "So, what is the plan for tomorrow?"

"Go to work."

She shot me a startled look. "Work?"

"I work at the local college as a janitor." I spoke up, knowing where the conversation was heading. "I'm not going to be gone the entire day. I'll have David or Goliath stop by tomorrow. You can reach me on the cell if anything happens."

"But why would you go there, with everyone after you?" She said slowly, like molasses pouring out.

"Because tomorrow I'm going to have eyes on me at all times, and I want them on me in a public place. It wouldn't be the best option for me and you to be constantly together tomorrow. I can't be with you at all times, but that doesn't mean I'm going to cut off all communication with you."

"Are you alive because they expect you to just hand me over?"

Not only did I tell her yes, but I went into the events that had happened after getting knocked out. I gave every detail of being tied up and the dilemma Chester had presented me with. I told her about Chester, leaving out nothing on Tony and how he had gleefully confessed to me his responsibility for Susan's death. At times, my tone turned to angry as I described how Tony was responsible for both Thelma's and Susan's deaths, too.

As I got to the end of my story, I started feeling calm, like someone had taken off some of the weights hanging on my back.

During the walk home I'd had the same thoughts, playing ping-pong with one player in my head. Until I had spoken my mind, though, I hadn't realized the extent of the emotions I'd been holding in. It was one thing to tell the guys or Johns what was going on, but to say the same things to Kathleen had a different meaning.

Kathleen never cut me off and I was thankful for it. But it wasn't like she was satisfied hearing the news. She gave me a determined look, but at times would look defeated, too. Whatever positive ideas were in her mind were met with claws and knives. The wide range of emotions showing on her face were the same ones my mind constantly gnawed. When she finally spoke, she made sure to keep a neutral tone.

"You know," she said, clearing her throat, "Susan always told me to get out of this town and explore the world."

I looked at her like she forgot where she was and who she was speaking to. It wasn't the reaction I'd thought she would have.

She continued, "Ever since we were kids, she would tell me there's a whole world out there for me. Did she explain to you she moved away for a few years before coming back here?"

I shook my head.

"She lived on the West Coast during that time, mostly for work, but when she came back, she constantly talked about how different it was out there. She described the ocean as if I'd never seen one, how you could walk through the forests for days, and how the people treated you differently. She made it sound like the West Coast was a different planet."

"Why did she come back?" I asked.

She shrugged. "She said it was because of a job offer she got here, but I could always tell it was for me. Yes, we were close, but I never wanted her to move back here because she felt like it was some family obligation. I wanted her to get out there and explore as much as possible. I wasn't like her; I didn't need to explore. I always thought my place was here."

"Are you trying to connect the dots so you can blame yourself? Don't bother, because it isn't true. Susan was an adult who made her own decisions. Your staying or going isn't anyone else's concerns but your own."

She hesitated. "But if she—"

"But if she wasn't here, then she wouldn't have died, right? She could've died in a car wreck back on the West Coast, or drowned in the Pacific, or been eaten by a bear. Tearing your mind apart on something you can't change isn't going to get us anywhere. We're here now and we have a lot on the line."

"I just wish she could have seen what her little sister was capable of doing."

When Kathleen said that, it reminded me of the journey I had been on and my determination to get to the finish line no matter how many landmines were buried.

"I only knew your sister for a brief time, but she wasn't the type who was selfish or only did things to benefit her own agenda. Every time she talked about you, she described you like no one else. Her fear of losing you was bigger than anything else she could handle. She pleaded with me to find you because she didn't care what it would cost just to know you were safe again."

The last part made me stop. All I wanted to do was bring Kathleen to Susan, and then tell Susan how she had been more than right. I would explain that Kathleen was uncovering one of the biggest scandals in the state's history. I would go into how Kathleen risked her life for something she wasn't even sure the world would accept. But most of all, I would tell Susan that I shouldn't have doubted her.

Kathleen looked at me, not saying a word, but waiting on me

to move the conversation along. Instead of making this about me and feeling sorry, I shifted the conversation.

"Susan reminded me so much of Thelma, my landlady who was brutally murdered. Both would've done anything for the people they cared about most. Sadly, it's not until they depart from this world that we realize what they meant to us."

Kathleen nodded. "How did Thelma support you besides renting you this place?"

"I was once a drifter, just making it by, day-to-day. At the time, I didn't see much use for anything besides just getting through each day. People didn't give much thought to me. When I met Thelma, she made me feel like I belonged in this town—like I had lived here my whole life." I spread out my arms. "People might look at this basement and the first word that comes to mind is 'condemned,' but I saw it as a home that I could come back to every day."

"They were there for us, and we didn't realize how lucky we were, right?"

I agreed.

Kathleen got up and walked around the couch. She stopped next to the record player, going through the box of records, one at a time.

She said, "While I was hiding out, I started going through your record collection. I had no idea you were into classical jazz. Were you always a jazz enthusiast or did you start listening to it recently?"

I got up and stood next to her. "As a kid, one of the few things I enjoyed about my father was his taste in jazz music. When he was sober, every night he put on a jazz album. You wouldn't think a child would want to listen to it, but I was thrilled any time he played his records. I wasn't allowed to touch them, so getting any chance to hear them was always a treat." A smile crossed my face.

"One of my favorite memories is seeing my father slow dancing with my mother in the kitchen to Miles Davis. The looks on their faces made me believe happiness was real."

I hadn't realized until then that she'd stopped going through the records and was looking at me. We gazed at each other for a few seconds before she returned to the records.

"Did any of these records belong to your father?" she asked.

I shook my head. "No. All of these I've collected over the years. I often go to yard sales or secondhand stores to find them. Ones like Jelly Roll Morton and Abbey Lincoln I had to search pretty far for, but I was able to track them down eventually."

"And is there one that you are still searching for?"

"I'm still trying to find Muddy Waters' *Folk Singer*. It was his second studio album and one that isn't exactly easy to find."

She nodded. "I know the album you're talking about. My favorite song from that album is 'Long Distance.'"

"You also listen to jazz?" I asked.

She smiled. "I don't just run around with stolen documents. When I was in college, I started listening to jazz after a course with a hyped instructor who couldn't escape the roaring twenties. I'd been a snob when it came to music, never believing there was any worthy music before the year 2000." She flipped threw a couple more albums before stopping and pulling one out. "Are you in the mood for some Thelonious Monk?"

"Who isn't?"

Kathleen meant everything she said as her hands carefully took the record out like it was an egg and settled it on the turntable. She moved the needle down with grace until it touched the record. The rhythm started to play after a brief moment. The first song was a soft rhythm, more of the laid-back kind.

Without saying a word, Kathleen and I looked at each other.

She put a hand on my shoulder while I put a hand on her hip. I cupped my other hand and she placed her free hand on top of mine. We started to sway to the music, slowly finding our bodies in sync with the trumpets and clarinets.

With the whole world outside ready to bust down the door and drag us away, there was no reason for us to be dancing at that moment, but the ease of the music and the softness of Kathleen's touch put my problems at ease. It seemed as if the world had disappeared.

Kathleen looked to be thinking the same things. She closed her eyes as a faint smile appeared. She breathed in through her nose, and then exhaled through her mouth like she was sitting cross-legged on a cloud. The longer I held her, the more I felt her muscles and her body relax. I could only imagine the last time she'd felt this serene. She opened her eyes and looked directly at me.

"For once," she said, "it's nice not to think about grabbing my stuff and going on the run."

"You took the words right out of my mouth."

We didn't say anything more as the music continued. We danced, letting our bodies succumb to the rhythms and putting us at peace. I spun her a couple of times and she laughed.

Just as the song was about to end, she leaned in for a kiss and I didn't hesitate to mirror the image. Her lips were soft. I put my hand behind her back and caressed her. She squeezed my shoulder. She then moved back from me with slight force, taking a few steps back, but still looking at me.

The music continued to play, but I couldn't tell you what song it was as Kathleen took off her shirt and dropped it to the ground. She had a white bra on, letting her hair cascade over half of her face. For a woman on the run and in hiding, she was surprisingly tanned. I stood in place.

"With the world ending for both of us," she said, "how about one more night before the guillotine descends on us?"

I didn't reply as she took a couple more steps back. As she got to the door of my room, she took off her bra and dropped it to the ground. I remained still as she reached behind her and touched the doorknob.

"Let's just help each other forget the bullshit," she said.

When I approached her, I lifted her up and put her back against the door. She wrapped her legs around me as she grabbed the sides of my face and leaned in to kiss me. I opened the door and carried her into the bedroom.

The music continued to play.

20

With only a few hours of sleep, I was already up and getting dressed. Kathleen was still asleep, the covers just above her shoulders. I made sure to be quiet, but my guess was Kathleen hadn't slept much in a while and a seven-point-zero earthquake wouldn't rattle her. She didn't seem like the type who needed a kiss goodbye for the day, but I still picked up her clothes off the ground and laid them on the bed before I left.

Outside, the sun beat down with force, but the weather was relatively cool. The morning dew was just about to burn out quickly as I scanned the area. A pin drop would make more noise than the silence that morning brought. Besides a few birds chirping and a Toyota Highlander that passed by, there wasn't any noise moving through the air.

I was about halfway to work when I spotted a brown Chevy following me. The vehicle had only been following me for a half mile, but I knew they were targeting me. There were two men in the car, both sitting in the front. The driver had on a pair of aviators, while his buddy stared at the back of my car like it was made of gold. They tried to blend with the other cars on the road, but their car looked like a giant turd on wheels. The only good thing I could pick up was that they were following me and weren't staked out back at the house. I pretended I didn't notice them as I drove the rest of the way to the college.

When I made it to work, Mr. Henderson gave me enough air to fill a blimp. To say he was angry was an understatement, but I had no excuse to build a defense. At times, he went red in the face, so much so that he became slightly dizzy. I stood there, unsure whether he'd fire me or if I should help him into his seat when he became too dizzy.

Neither happened.

"But I'm going to recommend to the administration that they put you on parole," he said.

I told him I understood and didn't argue with him or add anything to the conversation. Instead, I grabbed a mop and bucket and commenced with my shift.

I started out cleaning the bathrooms across the library. This would help me win back some points with Henderson, since those bathrooms were closest to the main exit and used more than any other bathrooms in the building. Also, I wanted to stay hidden from everyone as much as I could because I wasn't sure how much of my image from last night was uploaded onto the internet. I won't go into details, but it took me over an hour to clean up both bathrooms. This involved a couple of trips with a fresh bucket and several latex gloves. After I was done, I thought I deserved a medal for making it through without vomiting.

During my ten-minute break, I called directly to the rotary in the basement, making sure everything was all right on Kathleen's end. The phone rang several times, making me worried they'd found her, until she picked up.

"Truman?" she asked softly.

"It's me," I responded.

She took in a deep breath. "The problem with antique phones like yours is there's no caller ID. I can't remember the last time I was nervous answering one."

"I apologize for that, but thankfully it's not a number anyone knows, so that's why I called it. Maybe one day they'll bring back the rotary, but with caller ID." I straightened my shoulders. "I was just checking in."

"Was I really that good last night that you're trying to be my knight in shining armor now?"

Knowing I didn't want to use the little time I had left on break flirting, I changed subjects. I answered her question by explaining my drive in with the Chevy and its two occupants following me.

"Have you noticed anything strange there?" I asked.

"No," she said, her tone going serious, "I haven't noticed anyone lurking around the house, but then again, I haven't been outside and gotten a good look around."

"And you don't need to start now. No one should bother you while I'm out of the house, so hang tight until I return. There's plenty of food in the kitchen. I'll have an answer for you later about the files. Let me give you my number to this cell, just in case something happens."

"Another reason why smartphones have dominated."

"Yes, but you need to distance yourself from all electronics."

I gave her my cell number. We each said we would be in touch, just in case an emergency occurred, and then hung up.

I continued with my list of things that needed to be done, like taking out the garbage and moping the floors, but I always kept my main focus outside for the Chevy. Now and again, I went towards the front of the building where I could either get a look through a window or door to see if the car was around. The vehicle stayed towards the back, mostly out of sight so it wouldn't arouse any suspicion.

It was around noontime when my phone buzzed. Thankfully,

I was in the break room, sitting in a metal and plastic chair on the opposite side of the room from a pair of instructors who acted as if I wasn't in the room. David's name was on the phone screen.

"Everything okay?" I asked after answering.

"We're fine right now," he said, "but we think there might be someone outside watching the place."

My mind went back to the two passengers in the Chevy. It wasn't crazy for David or Goliath to believe in that theory. There was no doubt Chester and Edmund wanted all of their corners covered and tagged. Knowing Kathleen was currently safe at my place, it was time to turn my attention to the guys. They were the only ones who could crack the files before time ran out.

"What have you seen?" I asked.

"A black Ford keeps passing the apartment every ten minutes. Sometimes they park across the street, but they only stay for a brief time and then move on."

"Are you sure it's the same one?"

"Positive. Goliath confirmed it after getting the license plate."

No point in asking more questions. It took a little push for me to see that they were being watched. The sound in David's voice would pass any lie detector.

"I have an idea," I said. "I'm at the college now because I want to keep Edmund's people far away from Kathleen. You and David need to come to the college as well. Having you guys here will make it seem that we're going to have a meeting here with Kathleen. I want to keep them guessing until the files are leaked."

There was a moment of silence before David responded. "We can pack up a few items and meet you at the college library."

"And remember, you don't have to completely play the incognito game. Sell it to the Ford outside that you guys are keeping your heads low so they have a chance to follow you, but don't give them any ideas that you know they're staking you out."

He said he would, and then hung up.

Not only did I perform the minimum requirements of my job that day, but it felt like I had a new job of keeping out of sight from the general public. As the day emerged, more people looked at me like they had seen me before but couldn't place me. I could tell the events at the banquet hall were becoming more viral, so I acted like I had to urgent business in the janitorial closet or the garbage room.

But while I kept my face down from everyone, I kept expecting to see Tony or his reflection every time I either turned around or got near. He was out there, hungry with violence and using any excuse to pull the trigger again. There was no doubt he wanted to put me into the ground like his other victims. Chester was someone who could be controlled, but Tony loved nothing better than to spread his name around town using fear as a tool.

It was around one-thirty in the afternoon when I got a text message from David to meet him and Goliath in the library. I checked in with Henderson first, making sure everything was cool. When he didn't rip my head off, I kept moving towards the library.

When I stepped into the library, I had the same sensation as the first time I had met the guys. After entering, I knew they would be waiting near the computer area. When I reached the computers, I found them with their backs to me and faces buried in glowing screens, much like the first time we met to find a killer. Even though time had passed, they both had the same determination as they had then.

David turned to me as I approached. "Goliath isn't far from cracking everything."

"Haven't you slept?" I asked Goliath.

"Nope," he replied, without turning.

David continued, "My sources are ready for the files. I've been giving them breadcrumbs today, little by little, of what we've found so far to keep them interested. A number of them are growing irritated, feeling that this whole thing might be a farce."

"And the trip here?" I asked.

He grunted. "The Ford was definitely following us. I occasionally looked in the rearview mirror, but made sure not to stare. I listened to what you said and didn't drive crazy or anything to lose them. They followed us all the way here. The last I saw they were sitting towards the back of the parking lot."

"And did you happen to see a brown Chevy as you walked in?"

He shook his head. "I don't remember that, but I wasn't looking over the whole lot and taking down car specifics."

I didn't need to follow up with another question because I had a hunch the Chevy was still out there. Chances are they were having lunch with the Ford pursuers. I wouldn't have been surprised if I walked outside at that moment and found enough automobiles to fill a car show.

I looked around the library. Through the slits in a bookcase, I could see the library was relatively calm with just a few patrons minding their own business. There were enough people in the building to make anyone from the outside think twice about coming in and making a disturbance. David and Goliath are ninjas of blending into a crowd, and this was their mecca.

"Just keep digging as long as you can," I said to David. "If anyone gives you any hassle, let me know. And make sure to keep your phone on you at all times."

He said he would, and without any further reply, I left.

I felt like a caged hamster with the world peering at me as I walked the halls of the college, doing my best to act busy and avoid contact with everyone. It seemed time was both slowing down and speeding up at the same time. I took one of the brooms from the closet and marched into unoccupied rooms like there was a dust epidemic that had swept the building.

It wasn't until I noticed the sun starting to hide in the west for the day that it was time to call it quits. The faculty in the building was starting to leave one-by-one and the students were ready for the bars. Even Henderson saw me as he tried to leave.

"You're still here?" he asked with a surprised look. "This must be the first time in years I saw you stick around before I left."

"Just trying to do as much as I can get done before calling it quits."

He didn't seem impressed. "Fine, but I'm still going to recommend that management puts you on probation."

I said nothing as he put on his checkered fedora and walked towards the exit.

I wasted no time after Henderson left to change into my street clothes and then hurried back to the library. When I entered the library, there was no one left except the guys and a middle-aged woman behind the counter who looked ready to quit her job. I moved with some pep in my step over to the guys. Just as I got there, Goliath stood up like he had won the lottery and David tuned around like he was going to run but stopped when he saw me.

"I was just coming to get you," David said. "Goliath cracked the files."

My eyes widened. "Did he start sending the files out to everyone?"

"No," Goliath said, "I just broke through. I was about to start sending them out."

"What were you able to find? Is there anything about Thelma?"

Goliath nodded. "Yes. There are transactions in here about

Edmund's company illegally paying off most local, state, and federal government officials for specific properties. There's at least ten times more documents than the paper copies. When it seemed certain homeowners wouldn't budge, then there were cash payouts to third parties to perform the job, and as it says in documents, there were evictors. They would terrorize people with vandalism or outright violence. These were wire transfers to certain known criminals, who had never been employed by the company, at least for tax purposes. Thelma's name does come up several times as a person who refused to sell."

"But anything about the murder?"

He shook his head. "Nothing going that extreme, but there's enough bribery, embezzlement, and fraud to put Edmund and most of his company away."

It was frustrating to hear her murder wasn't among the many pages, but I had to bite my tongue and not let the look of disappointment show. Maybe I had been expecting a direct link to Edmund, pinpointing him as the murderer, but that was foolish. He wouldn't be that stupid and I should've known better. This was something the police could use as leverage against a person like Chester or anyone within the company to make them confess Thornton's involvement. I shook my head, tabling those thoughts for later.

"Can you upload the files remotely?" I asked.

He gave me a puzzled look. "I can, but it will take longer."

"We don't have much of a choice. It's starting to get dark outside and we need to move again."

"All right," Goliath said, "I have the files on my tablet, so I can start sending them out now."

"It wouldn't make sense for us to go straight back to our apartment, would it?" said David.

I shook my head. "It's better if we can stick together. I'm heading back to my place for Kathleen. We can decide if we need to go to another location when we get there. I want to make sure she's safe and that we get the files out early enough for law enforcement to kick in right away. I'll call Detective Johns on the road and let him know what we're doing. He can meet us."

We didn't say anything more as the guys packed up their gear and we started to move out. I felt we were going to get jumped at any moment, so I made sure to stay in front just in case someone did show and I had to give the guys as much time to escape as possible. Luckily, the halls were bare, making it easy for us to move fast. A few people passed us, but we made sure to keep our focus forward and not stop for any meaningless chitchat. When we got to the front exit, I double-checked to make sure the guys were ready to hurry to our vehicles.

When we pushed through the doors and made it outside, there were no signs of either the Chevy or the Ford in the parking lot. With the exception of a few vehicles, there wasn't any sign of life. We stood there for a moment, amazed by the silence. I expected triple the number of cars with a small platoon ready to take us. We snapped out of our surprise quickly and hurried to our vehicles.

On the road, I drove ahead of them, glancing back every minute to make sure they were the only ones following me. They traveled close to me, acting as if our cars were two magnets. Every time I looked past their car, I didn't see any vehicle that was suspicious. It started to make me paranoid, wishing someone was following us so I knew where they were.

I tried contacting Johns a couple of times while driving. The speaker on my cell rang several times until I got his voice message. For once, I was trying to get the big bastard and he wasn't picking up. I didn't bother leaving him a message, because I figured he would know something was urgent if I was calling him a number of times in a span of ten minutes.

With no traffic, we got back to my place fast and parked in front of the house. There was no point in trying to hide our cars. And just like the parking lot on campus, there was no one there except a quiet road and a flickering light from one of the lampposts. When we got out of our cars, we went straight for the front door, rather than sneaking around to the back.

Through the front door, the calm and silence made me uneasy. It was as if there was an invisible crowd in the room, all silently gazing at the three of us. The entire floor was dark and the only sounds were our footsteps. No one made an attempt to flip the switch. Goliath was the last to enter, forgetting to close the door behind him.

"Kathleen!" I said, projecting my voice towards the basement door.

Within a few seconds, I heard footsteps coming up the stairs, and then Kathleen appeared in the darkened room. She flipped the switch on the wall and the room illuminated.

"Any problems since I've been gone?" I asked.

She shook her head.

I turned to Goliath. "How are we doing with the files?"

He shrugged. "They're still being sent out, but going slower now."

"At least they're still going." I reached for my phone. "I'm going to try Johns again. Shut the door and—"

Out of the corner of my eye, I spotted the outline of two people standing on the porch. I was just about to make an attempt to slam the door when Longhorn and Johns both appeared in the light of the door frame. Bewilderment was written on their faces.

"I got your text to meet you here, Pierce," said Longhorn,

holding up his phone.

"I didn't send you a text message."

And that was when Longhorn was shot in the shoulder.

21

"MAN DOWN!" Johns screamed into his radio. "Request an ambulance and backup."

Johns moved Longhorn out of the way as I slammed the door shut and fell to the ground. Everybody scattered to different parts of the room as the door was riddled with bullets. Everyone either leapt to the side or hit the ground as multiple bullets went through the door and windows. I looked over as Johns pulled Longhorn over with him against the wall. Kathleen crawled over to them, applying pressure to Longhorn's gunshot shoulder. David and Goliath both crawled over to where I was, using their bodies to shield the electronics.

When the gunfire stopped, we all stuck to the ground as if more bullets were still going through the house. I looked around. Besides Longhorn, no one else was hit, but they froze in a statue-like state for a few seconds to assess the situation. The only noise was Longhorn moaning when Kathleen maintained pressure to his shoulder wound. Johns was the first to move, reaching for his gun at his side.

The bullet-riddled door was kicked in with force. Chester walked through with a smoking nine-millimeter Beretta. Johns wasted no time in pointing his gun at him.

"Put down the gun," ordered Johns.

Chester pointed his gun at me. "Put yours down, Detective."

"I'm going to give you to the count of—"

"Of what?" said Tony as he entered the room, "The count of three? I'll give you just one." He pointed the Colt towards Johns as he motioned to Longhorn. "Your buddy doesn't look like he can help out. You might get one shot off, but who are you willing to sacrifice before taking a bullet yourself?"

The gun in Johns' hand looked like it turned to stone as his hand started to shake. Sweat dripped onto his eyes and he blinked repeatedly. The slow realization of his defeat materialized on his face. With nothing more than a pair of fours against a full house, Johns dropped his gun to the ground.

"Smart," Tony said with a smile. "Now kick it towards me."

Johns did as he was told. When the gun neared him, Tony kicked it across the room with one swift kick, away from everyone. Johns repeated the same steps when Tony made him take Longhorn's gun.

Darren walked through the door, closing it behind him. He was the only one not carrying a gun. He studied the room for a brief moment, looking down at the victims like animals ready to be put down.

He said, "We don't have much time. A number of people are standing in their driveways and on their lawns, trying to figure out what happened."

Chester ignored Darren, instead casually walking up to me and the tech wizards. He had a look about him I imagine Death would have if it had a face. He put the barrel of the gun under my chin and lifted my head until our eyes locked.

"I didn't think I would get all your pals into one room," he said. He took out a phone from his pocket. "Cloning your phone was simple. I just needed you and the cops. I would take care of your friends later. But now I can clean house all at once...starting with you, Darren."

Everyone, including the intended victims, turned to a stunned Darren. He was about to speak when Tony grabbed him by the hair and threw him against the wall. Darren hit the wall with force, but he didn't fall to the ground. He had the look of someone who had gotten caught with someone else's wife. Darren's face grew more anxious the closer Tony moved towards him.

"You didn't think we knew about you, Darren?" said Chester. "Whatever slick ideas you had we were three steps ahead. We've been tailing you since shortly after Thelma's death. Tony knew you were getting soft. You're not going to give away any more secrets, like a rat, again." He nodded to Tony.

Tony lifted the Colt and pressed it against Darren's brown eye. He pulled the trigger and a deafening noise vibrated throughout the house, compelling me to turn away. When I turned my head back, I found what was left of Darren. I saw the mirror image of Thelma. Half of his face was gone and his green eye was looking directly at me. A full circle was formed.

"And the rat couldn't even decide on a set of eyes," Tony said, laughing.

Johns' face turned red, his body moving like he was going to make a play, but Tony pointed the Colt at him. Johns froze.

Chester pivoted to me. I knew I was next, that I wasn't going to walk out of the room, but I had to keep stalling as long as I could before backup showed. At least I could save everyone else in the room and they'd only take me out. Chester and Tony weren't going to just wait, though.

"Are you going to give me the files or do I start shooting?" asked Chester, waving his gun.

They didn't know about the growing number of people with

an internet connection receiving the files. I had to walk on eggshells, knowing full well that they would put us into our graves when they learned the truth.

"It's around, not far," I said.

Eerily calm, Chester pressed the gun against the side of my neck. "You've got five seconds before I randomly point and shoot someone."

I didn't say anything.

"You really want to sacrifice someone?" he asked.

"I would rather you just shot me. It doesn't matter if I give up the files to you now, because both options end the same."

Chester smirked. "We'll see. Tony, kill the bitch."

Tony grabbed Kathleen by her hair and yanked her up. He stood her in the same spot Darren had just occupied a few moments before. She stood in a pool of Darren's blood, a few feet away from his corpse. She was ordered to stand straight, but she kept shivering like her body was covered in ice water. Tony put the gun between her eyes and pulled the hammer back.

I opened my mouth as Johns screamed. We all turned as he got to his feet and charged Tony like a bull. In a panic, Tony aimed the gun towards Johns and fired. A hole the size of a fist ripped through the drywall behind Johns' shoulder. It didn't faze Johns as he turned into a linebacker, picked up Tony, and they both went through the front door.

Chester lowered his guard and gave me and the guys enough time to react. David grabbed his arm and was able to smack the gun away. Goliath lunged for Chester's legs, pinning him in place. I clenched my hand into a fist and sent it right into the middle of Chester's face. He went back, half of his body falling on Goliath.

A few gunshots rang from outside.

Chester picked up Goliath by his throat and threw him into

the kitchen. David tried to throw a punch to Chester's side, but ended up getting a fist to the stomach. Judging from how hard he got hit, I'd thought David was going to throw up.

Kathleen stuck with Longhorn in the corner, applying pressure on his wound. Kathleen kept her hands pressed on both the front and back of his shoulder, indicating the bullet had gone through. Longhorn tried to get up, but only made it a few inches before dropping back down. Kathleen forced him to stop moving so he wouldn't bleed out.

Chester's eyes searched for his gun, but instead found me staring at him. He smiled as he put his fists up and positioned his body into a fighting stance. I did the same—minus the smile. No gun was going to give either of us the satisfaction that our fists could. From the corner of my eye, I saw David going into the kitchen to check on Goliath.

Chester darted at me and threw the first punch. He missed, but barely. He was fast and I knew he'd kept up his training. I threw a punch at one of his kidneys. He reacted with discomfort, but my hand felt worse than his annoyance. I gave a one-two combo to his chest, but I could tell he wasn't going to go down easy. He shoved me into the kitchen where I found David helping Goliath to stand.

"Get whatever you can and sneak out the back," I quickly ordered them.

David opened his mouth, but I rushed back into the fight.

Just as I hit Chester in the chest, he hit me in the shoulder. I thought my arm was going to be crushed by the force. I didn't show any signs that the punch had made an effect and raised my arms. He smiled at me like he was trying to get inside my head, but I kept my face neutral and my emotions stoic.

It was difficult to tell if David and Goliath had made it out of the kitchen. Chester was half-blocking my view of the kitchen. I didn't hear anything coming from that area, so I assumed they'd made it out. I was just happy Chester kept his attention on me and not on going after the guys.

Chester had started to move faster, making it more difficult for me to either block or dodge his throws. Most were getting through to me and I knew the fight wasn't going to last much longer. I had to think more strategically.

My plan was to go for his head. It was risky, but I needed to end it quickly or he was going to break me quick. One of the first two punches I made connected with his ear. His skin started to bleed, but Chester acted like nothing had happened. When I tried again, he dodged it and I ended up with a punch to the gut.

The air deflated from me and I bent over slightly. I started to inhale when Chester punched me in the back, directly on my spine. It felt like my soul was shot to the moon. I wanted to howl, but I spun around and missed another punch. I stumbled a bit and went down to one knee. I looked up just as he raised his fist high in the air, ready to bring the hammer down on my head.

But just then, a glass vase broke over Chester's head. I glanced over and saw Goliath in a pitching stance.

For a few seconds, Chester acted like there were stars spinning around his head. This gave me enough time to give him an uppercut to the jaw. His head snapped back, causing his body to fall back a few feet. When his head pulled back up, I started to throw my muscle-weary fists into his face. I jabbed, I hooked, I power punched, whatever I could do in the small window I had left. I wouldn't allow myself to slow down just so he could find an opening.

He tried to throw a wild punch at me, but I grabbed his arm and twisted it roughly until I heard his shoulder pop. He cried out as both his knees dropped to the ground. With his nose broken and his teeth covered in blood, he started to scream. With a closed fist, I threw it across his face. His head finally hit the ground and he was out for the count. I checked his pulse and it was still pumping.

In the kitchen, David and Goliath stood by the cabinets. The determined duo hadn't taken my advice, and I was grateful for it.

"Stay with Kathleen and Longhorn," I told them.

Without hearing a reply, I stumbled out the front door. On the front lawn, I saw Tony completely flattened out. Johns, kneeling over him, had his hands around Tony's neck. Tony wiggled some, but Johns was on him like an anchor. Whatever fight it was, however brief it might've been, was over. Neither of them held a gun, but a quick search showed both of their weapons lying on the porch, away from everyone.

As I started to step off the porch, I heard the police sirens. The loud roar of multiple sirens coming in different directions meant they were only moments away.

Even with his face bloodied and teeth missing, Tony's smile said he would never break. You could tell he wanted to die, making sure he wouldn't be processed and thrown in a prison cell with the information he knew.

I approached Johns as he continued to strangle Tony. The sky could fall on Johns and he wouldn't notice. Johns was going to make sure all the anger, sadness, and rage would be taken away for good tonight.

I put my hand on Johns' shoulder and he stopped choking Tony. Disfigured, Tony breathed in a gasp of air. Johns made no sudden movements, nor did he turn around to see what had stopped him. Instead, he looked down upon Tony like a hungry animal spotting road kill. He breathed heavily, his body rising and then falling back to the earth.

The police vehicles showed, shutting down the road from

every angle so no one could leave or drive by, gawking. It appeared as if the entire police force was out, and it was one of the few times in my life I was excited to view that sight. At first, the headlights on the three of us seemed more powerful than the sun. The surrounding area was covered in red and blue lights.

After several seconds, still kneeling, Johns turned to me. He had tears rolling down his face and his red eyes looked like they had been maced. We looked at each other as he tried to focus.

"Truman, she's gone."

"I know, Detective," I said.

"No one has ever given a damn about me like she did."

I motioned to the crowd in front of us. "That's not true."

Johns looked ahead and saw several police officers of different identities and backgrounds standing shoulder to shoulder. They weren't shouting or making any verbal threats. They stood together and showed support for one of their own. Just like me, they had witnessed a broken man, someone they saw as one of their own in trouble.

Johns finally stood up. He looked around at the people he had worked with for so long and gave them a reassuring nod. They returned his nod.

"Okay, people," Johns shouted, "Detective Longhorn has been shot. I need the area secured and the paramedics here, now." He kicked Tony in the stomach. "And someone clean this shit off the ground."

22

We all regrouped at the hospital, beaten, broken, or both. The ambulance had gotten to the house seconds after the cops started to haul Tony away. I heard later that Tony and Chester were the last to be taken to the hospital together, and that all available ambulances had escorted us first. We were taken away to different rooms for the doctors to check on us, including David, Goliath, Kathleen, Detective Johns, and myself. We were quickly discharged when nothing life-threatening was diagnosed. Just prescriptions and an order for plenty of bed rest.

The big question came into the room with Detective Longhorn. He was rushed into the ER when he got there, but then we waited a long time before a physician informed us that Longhorn was going to be all right, but was going to need to spend some time in the hospital for recovery. We were all relieved knowing Longhorn was going to walk out of the hospital—with all limbs attached.

Even though the doctors had cleared us, we were interrogated by the police while Longhorn was still in surgery. Once again, we were split up and taken to different unoccupied rooms in the hospital for them to question us. They didn't see any point in dragging us down to the precinct, but they still needed answers to several questions that were burning holes into their case files.

Two detectives—a female and male—took me into a half-lit

breakroom to ask me their questions. I didn't hold back, letting them know everything. I figured they were going to find out the truth eventually; plus, I was too tired to play mind games. I explained to them the connection between Thelma's murder and Edmund's land empire. They mostly just transcribed into their notepads like they were writing a novel.

"You guys would be better off just going on the internet and finding everything I'm repeating to you," I told them.

About thirty minutes had passed before they told me it was enough. They made it clear for me to stick around town for a while so they could sort out all the details and information. As much as I needed a vacation at that moment, I told them I wasn't going to go anywhere.

David and Goliath were the first ones I ran into after my interrogation. They were standing by the vending machines, going back and forth with the same credit card in a late-night dinner. David was deciding between a bag of chips and a candy bar. As I walked up to Goliath, he was opening a bag of chips.

"Did the files finally make it out to everyone?" I asked him.

He enthusiastically shook his head. "Yes, during the ride over here. I've been checking my phone and have seen multiple posts spring up since about the files. People have been trying to reach out to me and David. I haven't responded to anyone yet."

"And it's best if you don't until you guys are calm and want to talk," I said.

David turned to me. "Were you already questioned?"

I nodded.

"They're now talking about jail time for us," he said with a worried face. "Edmund has been screaming at all local officials and law enforcement to take us in. He has little credibility left, but there are people who will still listen to him out of loyalty."

I shook my head. "Yeah, it seems like our legal troubles are about to begin, but our lives are still intact. You guys should work on getting our message out to as many people as possible, to make us sympathetic instead of the antagonists that Edmund'll call us so he can save himself. Get in touch with all your contacts and start spreading the truth to everyone."

"Yeah, we can definitely do that," David said with a pensive look on his face.

"But don't you think he'll just send more people after us?" asked Goliath.

"No," I said bluntly. "Edmund and anyone associated with him are now under a microscope. They won't be able to go anywhere or do anything without half of the world watching. All Edmund has left is his big mouth, and he will shout all the way to the International Space Station if it restores his image."

Neither said anything as they ate their high-sugar dinners. The way they ate their food with unnerving calmness told me that Edmund sending out ninjas or secret assassins wasn't high on either of their lists of possible retribution. I could tell they were slowly realizing I was right and that Edmund and his people weren't going to seek their physical harm for vengeance. It took them about a minute to eat what they could, and then they started collecting the bags they'd brought with them.

"You might want to go out the back," I told them. "A media circus is out front, and my guess is they have each of our pictures on their phones and computers."

David nodded in agreement. "Yeah, we'll head out the back. We'll go back to our place and get in touch with you when we can."

I told them I would be hearing from them soon.

David and Goliath each said goodbye as they did their best to stay incognito and snuck away.

Johns was the next person I saw. He was standing down the hallway near where the doctors were still operating on Longhorn. Johns was talking to a uniformed officer as I approached. Johns didn't appear to be questioning the officer, because he told the officer he would catch up with him later. It looked like he was trying some quick meditation when I reached him.

"They're saying Longhorn is going to be all right," he told me.

"Good." I had already heard the news, but went along with it.

"He'll be out of work for a while, but with enough physical therapy he'll be back to new—for the most part."

I gave him a nod of agreement.

"I heard you were already questioned."

"I was. They told me to stick around town for a while. Appears they're going to look into me, David, Goliath, and Kathleen. Edmund is demanding our arrests."

"Longhorn and I will make sure none of you will spend time in prison. Our testimonies will help solidify things, but it doesn't mean you won't face any repercussions. The cops I've talked to tonight aren't calling any of you guys villains. Once they clean up the body back at the house, they'll turn their sights on political figures, starting from this town and reaching out across both oceans."

We stood there for a minute, neither looking at the other nor pretending to make any acknowledgment. From a distance, we probably looked like two strangers whose battles had finally gotten to them. I stood with my back against the wall while Johns leaned forward a little, like he was going to pray. You didn't have to ask us what we were thinking or feeling; everything in our worlds was plastered on our faces. I almost forgot Johns was next to me until he exhaled.

"What you saw tonight, Pierce—" Every word came out meticulously, like he was specifically searching for the perfect ones.

"You don't have to explain anything to me."

He shook his head. "More like me explaining to myself what happened."

I said nothing. I understood what it meant to let the words out to cool down the body temperature.

He continued, "I would've killed him if you hadn't stopped me. Even with most of the cops showing up tonight, I still wouldn't have stopped myself. I would've made sure every breath of air escaped his body before everyone pulled me off of him."

I looked at Johns, making him aware had had my full attention.

"It feels like you're the only person who understands what Thelma did to keep us going." He lifted his shoulders and looked forward. "I always thought the world was filled with people like Thelma. But it's not. Until you lose that person you don't realize how scarce someone like that is in society. I had only seen pictures of Tony, so when I saw him in the flesh, acting as if a cherished person's life meant nothing, that's why all my reason went away."

"I built so much anger and vengeance this entire time that I didn't care how I would get Tony," I admitted. "I just needed him to pay, and I was ready to do whatever it took. When I saw you strangling him, I didn't see you—I saw myself. If it wasn't you, then it would've been me. I would like to believe I'm above violence, but give someone enough push and they're whole world can shatter."

Without saying more, Johns pushed himself off the wall and started down the hall towards a small group of uniformed officers. I figured he needed to walk the rest of the night and start scratching the surface of the things he had to work on. He got about a dozen steps when he turned and looked at me.

"You better clean up, Truman. You look like shit."

My mouth stretched into a grin as Johns turned back around and kept walking.

I walked in the opposite direction from Johns. What I wanted was to run away from that hospital and stay away from the rest of the human race for a while, but before I could, there was one person I had to see before leaving.

After aimlessly walking around for five minutes, I found Kathleen walking out of the bathroom. Her eyes were puffy, like she had been crying and couldn't stop. She hadn't changed her clothes, walking around in Longhorn's blood, her ruined shirt and jeans. Her disappointed face stared down at the redness on her hands. When she spotted me nearing her, she closed her eyes and shook her head like it was time to snap out of it.

"Damn blood can't come off," she said, rubbing her hands together. "I've washed them multiple times, but only some has come off. The movies make it seem like blood is made of water and falls right off."

"Disinfectant solution should do the trick."

She gave me a surprised look. "You're an expert in removing blood?"

"Let's just say it's happened to me enough."

I motioned to a couple of cushioned chairs sitting next to a closed door. We sat down and looked around for several moments, doing our best to people watch and act like nothing was bothering us. This rest was more for Kathleen than for me, so her mind could connect some dots just enough to keep her in the moment. Since she had been on the run from the first time I met her, it was strange to see her not moving frantically like her time was up in one place. She had the look of someone who had been on a rollercoaster for a week straight and was taking her first step off the ride.

"So," Kathleen said, looking back at her hands, "Longhorn is going to be all right." I wasn't sure if that was a question or a statement, so I treated it like the latter.

I nodded. "You helped save his life."

She tried to smile, but her eyes just blinked a few times.

I continued, "You don't have to worry about your safety. I've talked with a number of colleagues and Edmund and his people won't be coming after us."

She lowered her head and squinted. "For once, I wasn't worried about him or anyone else coming after us. His reputation is over; every TV here has been talking nonstop about him, but I didn't need them to tell me so. Working at the company for so long made me realize it was only built on a house of cards. You don't need to be an employee there to know the would-be empire has been dissolved.

I leaned towards her. "What are you thinking?"

It was a question I pretty much knew the answer to, but I still wanted her to say it. She knew what she wanted to tell me by the way she kept looking away from me and slowly rebuilding the wall around herself. The answer had been formulating fast since the events of earlier that night.

She inhaled deeply. "I need to finally take my sister's advice and spread my wings. Not exactly the circumstances I wanted to make this decision, but it's time for me to get far away and explore."

"Do you want to stay at my place while trying to figure out everything? The police will want you to stick around while things get sorted out."

She shook her head. "I'll grab my stuff tonight and head out to a motel. I need time away from everything and everyone." She tried to laugh, but it came out as a cough. "I've just found a loyal group of people I've connected with after being on my own for so long, and now I feel as if I'm running away from them."

"Everyone, especially me, understands you aren't running away. We're all going to be taking long vacations after this one."

Kathleen took my hand. Her hands cupped mine, making Longhorn's blood more glaring than before. She didn't raise her head until she found the right words.

"Truman," she said, "don't think what we have was just me being on the run. You were everything I had hoped for and I can't thank you enough."

"I didn't think otherwise." I lightly squeezed her hand. "The basement apartment should be unlocked and there hopefully won't be too much of a police presence there if you wanted to sneak back and grab your stuff."

"Thank you, Truman. For everything."

We stood up simultaneously as if our therapy session was over. She took one step towards the exit, but then turned around and kissed me. It was a soft kiss. It might've been for a few seconds, but it felt like an eternity. When she broke off from me, she gave me a smile that said the future was possible for either of us.

I watched as she walked through the exit.

And out of my life.

23

The rain had stopped over an hour before, but the humidity was prevalent by the time I reached the cemetery. When I walked past the stone-wall entrance, the area had a different feeling than it had when I'd been there before. Three months had passed since I was at the gravesite, but it felt like I hadn't been there in a decade. The oak and birch trees surrounding the cemetery looked as if they were gatekeepers to the dead. Walking through the cemetery, I treated the area like a minefield, making sure I stayed on the designated paths and didn't step on any markers.

When I got to Thelma's grave, the first thing I noticed was the freshly cut grass. The groundskeepers had done a good job of keeping up with clearing the area, but there were still a few leftover pieces of grass lying on top of Thelma's marker. Carefully kneeling to the side, I brushed off the grass.

As I looked down at her marker to read the years Thelma had been on the planet, it occurred to me she had seen and experienced so much, but I felt like I hadn't learned enough from her. This was one of the reasons why I wanted to visit her today.

I stood up and took my place at the foot of her gravesite. I looked down upon the marker and fresh-cut grass like I could see Thelma again. After a few seconds, I took out the picture of Thelma holding her baby nephew and laid the photograph gently next to her name. When I stood up, I took a deep breath.

"Thelma, I'm sorry it's taken me so long to get back here." I talked like we were back in the kitchen, with her going through the photo album.

It didn't matter if the cemetery was full of people, I was going to talk out loud to her like she was right here with me. There was so much that had built up inside of me over that past three months that I needed to tell her personally. I pushed my hand through my stubby hair like it was long and dangling in front of my face.

"First," I said, "I wanted to let you know about Edmund. Thelma, I really wanted to believe your nephew wasn't someone I thought about negatively. Now I understand why you never spoke of him. He's done evil things, but what he did to you I'll never comprehend." I lifted my face some and looked forward. "Even though he was caught, he's in a prison that might as well be a country club. I thought with the speedy trial he'd get a lengthy sentence, but the court found him guilty of fraud and embezzlement, giving him just five years in prison. Chances are he'll be out long before then with the appeal he has lined up. But the bigger issue was that I couldn't find the evidence connecting him to your death, and that is something I'll have to live with forever. His reputation and empire might've crumbled, but his biggest crime against you he won't answer for until he meets his maker in the afterlife."

"As for the man who sent your spirit away, Tony's trial is coming up and he's facing life in prison. Detectives Longhorn and Johns have created an air-tight case, with several eyewitnesses and a mountain of evidence to put him away for good. It's going to be difficult to see him in court, but I plan on giving a lengthy testimony to make sure every member of the jury understands that Tony's a great threat."

As I looked to my right and into the distance, I spotted a

middle-aged man and woman standing over a grave by a line of oak trees. The woman had a handkerchief covering half of her face and she leaned her head against the man's shoulder. He did his best to keep his back straight and be the person for her to cry on, but I could tell by his shaky legs that he wanted to keel over and have a breakdown. I didn't know whose marker they were visiting, but for some reason, I assumed it was their child. My brain just went there only by their posture and manners.

"Thelma," I said, looking back at her marker, "you created a lot of surprises in the past, but the house and money is on another level. I wanted to let you know that Edmund isn't going after anything you left me. It wasn't difficult after his arrest and everything falling apart around him. The point I'm getting at is that no one will be tearing down what you and your husband built."

"Which leads me into the next thing. I wanted you to be one of the first to hear that I'm starting my own private investigation firm. I'm calling it Thelma Reilly Investigations, and David and Goliath are on board. With the money you left, I'm going to use a good chunk to renovate the house and use as my office. I'm still going to live in the basement, but the rest I'm turning into a place where people can show up and feel like they are heard. Yes, I still have a ways to go to get my PI license, but now, thanks to you, I have a direction to aim for."

"When I first arrived in this town and met you, I didn't care much about what I was doing or about tomorrow. I wanted life to be simple because I didn't want to be attached to anyone, nor bear any responsibility except to myself. I thought I was doing myself a favor, but now I see my life having meaning because I chose to allow people in and gave myself purpose."

"I also quit the janitor position. Henderson seemed relieved by my decision, because he can hire someone who actually needs the job. We both were on good terms when I walked out of his office, because we both knew I needed change in my life."

My mouth shut when the next though popped into my head. I hadn't spoken about Kathleen since the last night I'd seen her in the hospital. When I got back home that night, she had taken her stuff and was already gone—true to her word. I knew our time had come to a close then, but I didn't know if there might be something down the road.

I gave myself a little time before I continued.

"During my search for your killer," I said to the marker, "I met someone. I know you would've liked her. She wasn't what I'd expected; I thought I was getting another person who was in over her head, but I found someone who had more backbone than me. But I can't cage a beautiful bird if she wants to go free. Maybe our paths will cross again someday; I'll let you know if they do."

Once again, I stood there for several moments, acting like a stubborn teenager who refused to say what they were thinking. I didn't want to spend an eternity just holding in what I had to say, but it was hard because it was criticism of Thelma that I knew I couldn't let go of until it was off my chest.

"I might not know how difficult things were for you, Thelma, but I wish you'd come to me with these problems. At first, I took it as someone of your generation who didn't go around spreading gossip, but I wasn't just anyone to you. You saw what I was able to do and that I would've done anything to help you. I still have so many questions, but I guess those are for the ages now."

"Anyway, I gotta get going to my community service. Me and the guys were able to make a deal with the District Attorney's office. The public had made it clear they didn't want to see me, David, and Goliath behind bars or they would riot. There are advantages to the internet, I guess. There was enough public outcry that the prosecutors didn't want to run the gauntlet. Even better, we were able to get the charges against Kathleen completely dropped. I think that's why I have no problem picking up trash on the side of the road every Saturday for the next two months."

I nodded several times like it was time to hang up the phone. "All right, Thelma, before I go, I wanted to say that I'm going to do a better job of stopping by more often." I wiped away a few tears. "Thank you."

Before I left, I took one more look at the middle-aged couple. The man was brushing off the marker, much like what I had done with Thelma's. The woman still had the handkerchief covering the lower half of her face like she was going to be sick. With her legs wobbling, I thought she was going to fall down, but the man stood back up and put his arm around her.

As I walked out of the cemetery, I felt like a big weight had been taken off me. Talking to Thelma had given me better insight into the direction I was heading and helped minimize the inner demons that had a firm grip on me. The temperature felt like it rising with each step I took. When I got back to my car, I started to open the door, but stopped myself and looked around.

On the horizon, a line of thunderstorms was heading my way.

Acknowledgments

Thank you to the staff at Apprentice House Press for letting me continue the story of Truman Pierce. It has been great to continue working with a well-respected publishing house that lets me tell the stories I want and supports my decisions.

To my parents and family. Thanks for being patient with me as I got through months and months of preparing the book and meeting deadlines. Your love and support have pushed me, not just being a better writer, but also a better person.

And thank you to my editor, Melanie. You have been a great teacher for me. Our conversations have only made me into a better writer. Here's to our continued friendship and mentorship.

About the Author

Patrick B. Simpson is the author of three novels. He is the creator of the Truman Pierce series. He is also the author of *Absolution*, published in 2025. He has published short stories in publications such as *Guilty Crime* and *Mystery Tribune*. He is a member of the Maryland Writers' Association. He currently resides in Montgomery County, Maryland.

Apprentice House is the country's only campus-based, student-staffed book publishing company. Directed by professors and industry professionals, it is a nonprofit activity of the Communication Department at Loyola University Maryland.

Using state-of-the-art technology and an experiential learning model of education, Apprentice House publishes books in untraditional ways. This dual responsibility as publishers and educators creates an unprecedented collaborative environment among faculty and students, while teaching tomorrow's editors, designers, and marketers.

Eclectic and provocative, Apprentice House titles intend to entertain as well as spark dialogue on a variety of topics. Financial contributions to sustain the press's work are welcomed. Contributions are tax deductible to the fullest extent allowed by the IRS.

To learn more about Apprentice House books or to obtain submission guidelines, please visit www.apprenticehouse.com.

Apprentice House Press
Communication Department
Loyola University Maryland
4501 N. Charles Street
Baltimore, MD 21210
Ph: 410-617-5265
info@apprenticehouse.com • www.apprenticehouse.com

www.ingramcontent.com/pod-product-compliance
Lightning Source LLC
LaVergne TN
LVHW010613100826
845148LV00014B/2954
* 9 7 8 1 6 2 7 2 0 6 6 9 3 *